'Help. You must help us, C — a muffled voice coming up from the region of his shoes. 'Cousin, it was like prayers answered when we saw in the papers that it was you who was coming to England. Like prayers answered.'

In spite of the ridiculousness of his position, Ghote could not restrain a thrill of pride at these words. In the papers. So his name had been there in the papers of this great city.

'Cousin,' the voice at his feet jabbered muffledly on, 'I have waited for every flight from Bombay. My wife insisted . . . My restaurant. Such trouble. Those waiters they know nothing, and they cheat.'

The plump little hands were pawing away at the bottoms of his trousers.

'Get up, get up,' he said furiously.

The bullet head, with its Gandhi cap still jammed in place, twisted round. Two big, bloodshot eyes looked up at him.

'Cousin, will you help?'

In the distance, Ghote saw, the bobby had swung majestically round and was now slowly approaching them.

He drew in a sharp breath.

'If there is some small way . . . ' he said.

Vidur Datta came shooting up to his feet like a fat cork released from the depths.

'Blessings on you, Cousin. Blessings on you. You have saved us. Saved.'

'Please,' said Ghote harshly, 'how old is the girl in question?'

'Seventeen, Cousin, Seventeen.'

Ghote's heart sank. The very worst age.

INSPECTOR GHOTE HUNTS THE PEACOCK

H. R. F. Keating

MYSTERIOUS PRESS

Mysterious Press books (UK) are published
in association with
Arrow Books Limited
62–65 Chandos Place, London WC2N 4NW

An imprint of Century Hutchinson Limited

London Melbourne Sydney Auckland
Johannesburg and agencies throughout
the world

First published in Great Britain by
William Collins Ltd 1968
Reprinted 1985 by Constable & Company Ltd
Mysterious Press edition 1988

Printed and bound in Great Britain by
Anchor Brendon Limited, Tiptree, Essex

ISBN 0 09 957960 X

One

Inspector Ganesh Ghote, of the Bombay C.I.D., stepped out of the narrow rubber-lined doorway of the big aircraft on to the platform top of the boarding-steps. He took in a deep breath of cold air.

So this was England. London. He was here, under an English sky. Unexpectedly, almost mysteriously it had seemed at times, but here.

Briefly he considered the situation which a whirlwind of events had plunged him into. It was a new departure in more ways than one. That was certain. Would he be able to carry out what he had to do in the way it ought to be done? There was no doubt about it: the responsibility of it all was as heavy as it could be.

And there were aspects of what lay ahead which he would just not let himself think about at this moment. He would have enough immediate problems in any case, without trying to jump impossibly high fences before he came to them.

He took a rapid look all round.

Above, grey clouds, huge and ragged, but somehow cool and unmenacing as they never were at home, were moving majestically across the low dome of the sky.

At his feet, the immense airfield stretched out, incredibly green. Darkly, damply and sombrely green. But, for all the dank atmosphere, the scene was one of tremendous activity, busy, purposeful activity. Dotted here and there over the huge extent of level grass, other aircraft were loading, unloading, taxi-ing, taking off, already coming in to land when they themselves had hardly touched down. Everywhere animation, precision and orderliness.

So much happening, he thought, so many people

`coming to this great metropolis, so many people leaving on missions to all the ends of the world. And he was among them, with his task to perform too.

Inside the enormous overcoat in bright green-and-yellow check, which his wife had given him as a parting gift to protect him from the unknown rigours of the English winter, he shivered a little.

Behind, the next passenger nudged him forward. He quickly descended the grey rubber-covered treads of the boarding-steps.

At their foot he cast a quick glance back at the great aircraft. Somewhere inside it still was his suitcase.

He frowned.

But there was nothing he could do but dutifully follow the straggling line of his fellow passengers into the little bus waiting for them beside the plane. He settled himself in a vacant inside place on one of the utilitarian-looking seats and turned to the window.

He wanted to see as much as he could as quickly as he could, to get himself as fully as possible into possession of every aspect of his novel situation before the moment that he would be called on to take steps for himself. Because it was important, he told himself, not to put a single foot wrong if he could possibly help it.

And everything was strange to him. He had had his long-nurtured impressions of what England was like, of course. But they were bound, he knew, not to match up exactly to the realities. The fazed view through the binoculars would need to be rapidly brought into focus.

He smiled a little to himself at the realisation that already one fanciful expectation had been falsified. Somehow, without at all clearly reasoning out how, he had thought he would step from the plane to be immediately confronted with the sight of the history-steeped pinnacles of the Tower of London, with the majestic spread of the mighty Thames rolling before it, with the ancient Houses of Parliament and sonorous Big Ben – heard often on the radio, now actually to be looked at –

with Westminster Bridge and all that the poet had seen from it.

And instead there had been this other Britain, this communications centre of the modern world, this place where things were really happening.

And the smile faded from his face. This was the Britain where he had come to play his part. And that part might begin at any moment.

The mini-bus was moving swiftly now across the great green expanse of the airfield, slipping under the wing of a huge BOAC jet painted in proudly regal colours, going straight towards a group of low, cleanly modern-looking, white buildings.

Ghote bit his lower lip.

The bus pulled up, quietly and efficiently, in front of a concrete archway. The more knowing passengers quickly got up and made their way into it. Ghote followed them, keeping his eyes skinned.

Ahead of him people had already begun to queue at the high desks of the immigration officers, their passports at the ready. Ghote dived into the unfamiliar recesses of his enormous coat and located his own brand-new passport. He brought it out and held firmly on to it.

He noted with pleasure the orderliness of the queue in front. This was the England he had expected. No one shouting, no one arguing, no one pushing stridently forward. Everywhere calm, order and dignity. He breathed a great contented sigh.

'Will passengers on Air India Flight 504 from Bombay now go to the Customs Hall. Thank you.'

The voice of the loudspeaker was unflurried, efficient, almost completely audible.

In the scrupulously clean, pleasantly warm Customs Hall, with a long broad bench running all the way down it manned by politely attentive Customs officers, Ghote saw, with an uprush of relieved joy, a big mechanical luggage chute, already clanking quietly away to itself.

So his case, unexpectedly whisked off at a distant,

distant Santa Cruz airport at the moment of departure, was to be reunited with him after all.

He went over and stood behind the more thrusting of his fellow passengers who had already assembled at the foot of the chute, looking impatiently upwards. Almost at once a variety of baggage began making the smooth descent towards them.

And abruptly Ghote found himself wishing his case had got lost after all.

With a growing feeling of hot shame, he saw that every single piece of luggage that had so far appeared was infinitely more respectable in appearance than the big, light brown, rather cardboardy – no, very cardboardy – suitcase which he had until that moment been so anxious to see again. It had served well enough back at home on their infrequent family holiday trips, and, in fact, it was much better looking than a great deal of the other luggage which had cluttered up the familiar platforms of V.T. Station as they had waited to go to the cool of the hills at Nasik. But in the international atmosphere of the airport here . . .

But remorselessly it appeared. And it looked worse than he had imagined, even. Standing slap-bang next to an extremely slim, smoothly zipped, special airweight case in an elegant shade of dark green, its hideous orangey-brown colour, masquerading as the tan of leather, stood out like an over-dressed travelling acrobat, garish through the dust-layers, glimpsed momentarily beside the wife of a rich businessman, cool and aloof in immaculate silk sari.

Implacably the two cases slid down cheek by jowl towards the foot of the chute. Ghote glanced round. There were not many other passengers waiting now. If he stood back a little, perhaps everybody else would collect their baggage and he would be able to grab the case after they had moved to the Customs counter.

He turned away and began airily looking round the hall. But there was nothing there which he could reason-

8

ably be imagined as devoting more than one instant's attention to.

He flicked a quick look at the chute. His case had reached the bottom of the incline and had come to rest on the platform there. Luckily its super-elegant neighbour had been claimed by somebody's porter. But there were still more than a few passengers waiting.

He hit on the notion of feeling in the pockets of his enveloping check overcoat, as if there might be something he wanted to get hold of, his keys perhaps, before going to claim his luggage.

For what seemed minutes he stood conscientiously exploring the many pockets that seemed to be dotted here and there among the immense thicknesses of the new coat. But at last he came to the end of them all and had to look at the foot of the chute once more.

The situation hardly seemed to have changed at all. Baggage was still descending the incline in clumps of two or three items, and passengers and porters were still awaiting its arrival.

And then one of the porters actually seized the hideous orange-brown case and held it high aloft.

'Any gentleman own this?' he shouted. 'Any gentleman own this case? Would they kindly take it, please.'

Ghote marched forward.

'I think it is mine, thank you,' he murmured.

But the porter, holding the case above him in two large, meat-red, cupped hands, did not hear. He swung all the way round in a complete circle, looking out over the heads of the surrounding passengers for anyone likely to own such a disreputable object.

Ghote felt through and through the absolute contrast between the case – bulging, knocked about, hideous in colour, pathetic in its attempt to pass itself off as a genuine article – and his surroundings, quietly modern, smoothly efficient, clean beyond belief, warm and well-lit.

'Please,' he said, with something that turned almost into a squeak of agony in his voice, 'please, my case.'

'Ah. Very sorry, sir. There all the time, were you? I'll take it over to the counter for you.'

And the porter – tall, genial, magnificently above petty preoccupations, it seemed to Ghote at that moment – swung the abominable object easily off and laid it, with considerate gentleness, in front of one of the neat, business-like, calm Customs officers.

In the twinkling of an eye the case was examined and had bestowed upon its battered side a swift chalk mark of approval. Ghote lugged it off in the wake of the other passengers, unable to prevent himself comparing the process it had just undergone with the scenes of interminable delay and frustration he had occasionally witnessed down at Ballard Pier in Bombay when a big passenger liner had docked and the white-uniformed Customs officers there had filled in their innumerable forms and held fast to their innumerable rules.

He came out into the Arrivals Hall, a long, glittering, high-roofed, smooth-floored place, alive with clustered groups of passengers and their friends from every country in the world, talking animatedly, moving from place to place, contented and well-dressed.

Ghote stood near the doors through which he had emerged, looking on at everything. Who would have come to meet him, he wondered. They had said he would be contacted on arrival and given full instructions. Who among all these people had come to meet him?

His wandering gaze ran over the neat stacks of luggage left here and there along the huge length of the hall. Totally unguarded. This was the England he had so often dreamed about: the land of law and order, of honesty and respect for private property, of decent standards of living for one and all.

There were no beggars here, crouching by the doorways or propped against the masterful, airy grey stone staircases leading to the upper gallery of the big building. Here there was no continual whining of supplication and entreaty. Instead everywhere in the bright windows of the

10

various little shops, in the clean-swept huge area of the grey-and-white chequered floor, in the poised glittering clusters of lights – there was brightness and order. The brightness of the new and most modern: the order formed out of long years of constant endeavour.

And here he was, in the middle of it all.

He took another long, savouring look all the way up and down the great length of the hall. And then he saw him. Stepping in through one of the heavy glass exit doors, nothing more nor less than a British bobby.

Ghote stood and stared.

The figure in front of him really seemed to be exactly as he would have expected. He was all the pictures he had seen over the years come to life. Tall, loftily calm, helmeted, grave, clad from head to foot in dignified blue, he stood surveying the crowd before him with quiet aloofness.

And he and I are of the same fraternity, Ghote thought. We stand for the same things. He as a member of the legendary British police forces, myself part of a strong branch of that noble stock.

He felt a strong temptation to go up and speak. He could ask him the time, and then go on to mention casually that, for all the simple, inconspicuous, English-style overcoat he wore at this minute, he was a policeman too. He would sink the difference in rank, in the circumstances.

But there was that big, modern-style clock with its hands moving smoothly round, plainly and obviously right to the second. He would have to think of some other opening. And he would have to think quickly. The bobby was moving steadily in his direction. In a moment or two he would have gone inexorably by. And he must have a word or two, if only to see what he was really like.

Could he ask him whether he had seen anyone waiting to meet him? Yes, that would do.

He moistened his lips.

'Is it Ganesh Ghote?'

With a loud blast of sound, a man had burst to the surface immediately in front of him, eyes white and wide in a dark Indian face.

'Yes – '

'At last. At last. At last I have found. She is dead. Dead. You must help. You are the only one who can help us now.'

'But what – '

'Your niece. She is dead. Murdered. Killed. Assaulted.'

Ghote looked down at the face thrusting up at his.

It was solid and fat-packed beneath the white Gandhi cap jammed firmly on the bullet-like skull. The figure beneath it was plumply solid too, with the stomach protruding hard against a skimpy overcoat worn over baggy trousers.

'Who are you?' Ghote asked sharply. 'What is this you are saying?'

The mouth in the solidly plump face gulped open.

'But, Cousin,' the man said, 'I am Vidur Datta. Your wife's cousin's husband, Cousin.'

Ghote remembered. The full extent of his Bengali wife's family was always something of a mystery to him, but Protima had told him that she had a cousin in London whose husband had left their native Calcutta to start up a restaurant. She had told him to visit them if he could.

He frowned.

'But what is this about a niece of mine?' he asked.

'Oh, Cousin, she is not your niece. She is my wife's niece.'

'Well?'

'And, Cousin, she is missing from home.'

'Missing? And did you say dead?'

The blubber-firm shoulders under the tight overcoat shrugged.

'Who can tell, Cousin? All that is certain is that she has been missing from our home. Missing for three whole weeks.'

12

'I see, I see,' said Ghote calmingly. 'I am sorry that we should meet in such circumstances, Cousin.'

But his words had exactly the opposite effect from what he had intended. Instead of being appeased, the solid face in front of him looked thunderstruck.

'Cousin,' Cousin Vidur exclaimed, 'you are not going to help?'

'Help? What help can I give?'

An extraordinary suspicion blossomed in Ghote's mind.

'Listen,' he said, 'surely you have told the police here of this?'

'Yes, yes,' Cousin Vidur reassured him. 'But what have they done? Nothing.'

'What do you mean "Nothing"?' Ghote said sharply.

'But nothing. They have done nothing. If it is Indian involved in any matter, the police here do not care one little fig. Only for the licensing laws do they care.'

At this noisy denunciation, Ghote could not help glancing quickly round to see where the tall, helmeted figure of the bobby was. What if he had heard? What would he think of a fellow officer countenancing such talk? But he seemed safely far away, standing looking calmly round at the various people ranged about the glinting, grey-and-white floor of the long hall.

Ghote brought his attention back to the plump figure in front of him.

'Please tell,' he said, 'exactly what action the police took when you reported the matter.'

He had had experience of similar cases himself. They were as tricky as any in the book.

Vidur Datta wrinkled his stubby nose in disgust.

'They came,' he said. 'When we telephoned the police-station, they sent. But they sent woman policeman only.'

'And did she ask questions?'

'Questions she asked, and too many. Everything she wanted to know. Even private matters completely.'

'And she looked at the girl's belongings?' Ghote asked.

'Into everything she poked and pried.'

'That is just what I would expect,' Ghote said with coldness. 'And what happened after?'

'Nothing. She told she believed Ranee had run away only. She said she would enter on list of missing persons. And then nothing. For three weeks nothing.'

Suddenly the plump form in front of him doubled forward, and before Ghote realised exactly what was happening he found that his feet were being weepingly embraced.

'Help. You must help us, Cousin,' he heard the muffled voice coming up from the region of his shoes. 'Cousin, it was like prayers answered when we saw in the papers that it was you who was coming to England. Like prayers answered.'

In spite of the ridiculousness of his position, Ghote could not restrain a thrill of pride at these words. In the papers. So his name had been there in the papers of this great city.

'Cousin,' the voice at his feet jabbered muffledly on, 'I have waited for every flight from Bombay. My wife insisted . . . My restaurant. Such trouble. Those waiters they know nothing, and they cheat.'

The plump little hands were pawing away at the bottoms of his trousers.

'Get up, get up,' he said furiously.

The bullet head, with its Gandhi cap still jammed in place, twisted round. Two big, bloodshot eyes looked up at him.

'Cousin, will you help?'

In the distance, Ghote saw, the bobby had swung majestically round and was now slowly approaching them.

He drew in a sharp breath.

'If there is some small way . . . ' he said.

Vidur Datta came shooting up to his feet like a fat cork released from the depths.

'Blessings on you, Cousin. Blessings on you. You have saved us. Saved.'

'Please,' said Ghote harshly, 'how old is the girl in question?'

'Seventeen, Cousin, Seventeen.'

Ghote's heart sank. The very worst age.

Vidur gazed up at him with a new earnestness.

'And, Cousin, she was beautiful. Beautiful. A creature of brightness.'

'And not a word of any sort has been heard?' Ghote asked.

'Not one word. And, Cousin, you do not know London. It is a dangerous place, an evil and wicked place.'

'All cities are dangerous places for young girls,' Ghote replied.

He did not like to hear London, the distant source of so much of what he had cherished, the proud city he had at last set foot in, talked of in such terms.

Vidur looked at him with solemnity.

'Girls like Ranee can be killed by evil and sex-obsessed men,' he declared.

'And they can also leave home for the very slightest of reasons,' Ghote answered. 'I tell you I do not really see that there is anything I can do which the police here cannot do much better.'

'The police,' Vidur exclaimed with a new access of loudness.

He drew breath to launch into a redoubled tirade.

Ghote cursed himself. The police were the one subject he should have avoided. The bobby seemed to be heading straight towards them at this very moment. Was he coming to quell the disturbance? What a difference from the conversation he had imagined only a minute or two earlier.

'Look,' he said rapidly, before Vidur could take wing. 'Look, I will come and see you.'

'Cousin, you must stay. My wife insists. You must stay with us while you are here. You must be our guest.'

'Well, I will come and hear more about it. I will come this evening, if I can.'

15

The constable was almost on them, and Vidur was still half-pawing at his front and looking completely bereft of any sort of dignity.

Ghote twisted away.

'However at this moment I have other business,' he said. 'Important business.'

But Vidur was not so easily disposed of. He made a lunge at Ghote's arm.

'Excuse me, sir.'

It was the bobby.

Two

Ghote stared up at the aloof, distantly inclined face of the bobby, with every coherent thought suddenly expelled from his mind. That this should happen. Within minutes of his arrival in the England he had so long dreamt of, to find himself embroiled in an unseemly fracas and attracting the attention of a passing police constable, it was more than he could grapple with.

'Excuse me, sir. Are you by any chance Inspector Ghote of the Bombay Police?'

The words, sounding far off amid the whirl of his thoughts, brought a sudden cool floodlight of illumination.

Of course. How ridiculous. The bobby had been sent to find him. He must be attached to the reception party.

But why, oh why, had Cousin Vidur chosen just the very moment when he was being sought out to make that ridiculous, undignified, over-emotional, un-British scene? The constable could not but have heard and seen. At the very outset of the visit he had become a figure of fun.

16

He shook his head angrily.

In the meanwhile the constable had been saying something. And, what with this turmoil of thought and the noise above him from a sudden loudspeaker announcement in some language which sounded like Portuguese or Spanish, he had not properly heard. It had been something about someone waiting outside to meet him officially, and that there were cars there. But who it was and what his standing was, he had entirely failed to grasp.

He frowned in bewilderment.

'So if you'll excuse me, sir,' the constable added, with a trace of patient emphasis in his voice, 'I have one or two other gentlemen to look out for. The cars are straight through that door there, sir.'

And with a respectful nod he turned gravely round and marched off, solemnly looking from one group of travellers to another.

Ghote decided to head for the door the constable had pointed out while at least that was clear in his mind. In his present state of confusion, he thought bitterly, he would end up by picking on the wrong exit if he let things go any longer.

He hefted up his hideous, bulging case and darted a brief look at his encumbrance of a family connection.

'Good-bye then, Cousin,' he said hastily. 'I will see you this evening. Or later. But soon, quite soon.'

And, as fast as the weight of the case would let him, he made off in a beeline for the swinging glass double-doors he had kept his eyes fixed on.

But who was it that he was going to meet? He wished to goodness he had caught the name. Or the rank. The name or the rank. What sort of a person was it likely to be?

Beyond the doors, Ghote found that it was already beginning to get dark. It was the slow northern twilight he had read so much about. Tall lamps on high, elegant concrete standards had been lit, and under their orangey glare he saw three dark blue, well-bred police cars drawn up at the kerb of the broad pavement, each with an impassive uniformed driver at the wheel.

In front of the row of cars stood an elderly-looking, thin-faced man, emerging with something of the doubting aspect of the tortoise from a very stiff fawn-coloured trench-coat. He was standing vigorously rubbing his woollen-gloved hands together, as if only by the most violent action could he hope to keep their circulation going in even a rudimentary manner.

There was no one else at all on that particular stretch of pavement, and Ghote did not doubt that this was the person who had come to greet him. But who was he? That was the question. Vague hopes that he might have been in uniform, and could then safely have been called 'Inspector' or even 'Superintendent' had died the moment he saw him. In fact, he looked more like a sergeant, a detective-sergeant at the fag-end of a hard-working career, mostly concerned with some sort of laborious research work.

Ghote decided there was nothing for it but to confront him. He marched up, let his heavy case drop on the ground beside him, and thrust out his hand to be shaken.

'Good evening,' he said, 'I am Inspector Ghote, from Bombay.'

The thin, elderly-looking face lit up with a smile of notable sweetness.

'Ah, good. Good. The constable found you all right then?'

But never a word of self-introduction.

'Yes, yes,' Ghote agreed heartily, still shaking the rapidly ungloved hand. 'Yes, he picked me out without much trouble, I think.'

'Splendid.'

The tortoisy-looking man drew himself up a little inside the creaking, stiff trench-coat.

'May I,' he pronounced, 'offer you a most hearty welcome, on behalf of the organising committee of the Emergency Conference on the Smuggling of Dangerous Drugs, to that conference.'

He let his shoulders droop a little once more, and busied himself in forcing his long fleshless fingers back into their knitted glove.

'And, of course, on my own behalf,' he added.

'Thank you, thank you,' Ghote said formally.

Then, warming suddenly to the friendly twinkle in the elderly man's eyes, for the first time since setting foot on English soil he relaxed into a full grinning smile.

'Yes,' said his host, whom he had almost definitely pigeon-holed now as a long-service detective-sergeant, 'the powers-that-be are more than a little worried about drug smuggling, what with the Press making a great to-do every day and questions down in Parliament and all that.'

The words gave Ghote another thrill of excitement. Questions in Parliament. There in the Mother of Parliaments they would actually be debating the very business that had brought him hurrying so suddenly across ocean and continent to this legendary city.

He summoned up his gravest expression.

The sergeant rubbed his gloved hands together with an even more anxious vigour.

'So there was only one thing for it they decided,' he said. 'To call together everybody who could possibly help in the matter, and to try and get the whole business sorted out from top to bottom.'

'It was a very urgent decision then?' Ghote asked, out of a sense of politeness.

'Oh, yes. Good gracious me, it was. That's why you'll find yourself going to meetings at a number of rather out-of-the-way places. But nobody can get conference halls just for the asking in London. Too many people got their claims in.'

The vision of all the different meetings attracted to this great metropolis for their different purposes swelled up in Ghote's mind. He squared his shoulders under the bulky tweed of his new coat. He was one of these multifarious delegates, playing his appointed part alongside the thousands of others.

'It will not matter at all where we meet,' he said. 'The meetings themselves are the thing. It is the people there who will get the work done.'

'Quite so,' the sergeant said, a little tersely. 'And at least everybody asked is coming – except your Number One, of course.'

The sudden reminder that he himself was the merest of substitutes at the Conference abruptly sobered Ghote. His mind went back to the moment, a bare four days ago, when he had been summoned out of the blue to report to the huge J.J. Hospital where Superintendent Ketkar, Director of the Narcotics Branch, under whom he had been serving for a short while past, was lying disabled by a broken hip.

He remembered feeling a good deal of perplexity as an Anglo-Indian nurse trotted on clicking heels in front of him to the door of the white-walled, bright private ward. Why should he be ordered to report to the superintendent when there were two perfectly good deputy superintendents busy running the branch? It was highly mystifying.

Superintendent Ketkar was lying on a very high bed propped up on a dozen pillows arranged in a great plump fan behind him. His body protruded from a thick cylinder of plaster covered by a heavy cotton-weave white counterpane, neatly folded back. He looked utterly helpless.

The sight was a decidedly unexpected one for Ghote. Superintendent Ketkar was in the ordinary way one of the least helpless men he had ever encountered. He had had a career in the police like the massively inevitable rise of a space-rocket from its pad. It had brought him now to the head of a recently established branch set up to deal with the growing international problem of narcotics, in which in a short time he had earned himself world-wide acclaim.

All this blazoned itself out of a striking, hawk-like face set on a formidably erect body – in the ordinary way.

But Superintendent Ketkar had slipped on a strip of mango peel. And now in this high hospital bed he resembled nothing so much as a wooden puppet with a vital string snapped.

But he still wasted no time.

'Inspector,' he had said, without asking Ghote to sit down on the high-backed, cane-seated chair beside the bed, 'I want you to go to England.'

'Very good, Superintendent.'

Long training helped Ghote to produce the words. But internally he could do nothing but ask himself in a chaotic whirl whether the superintendent had actually said what he seemed to have done.

'My friend Detective Superintendent Smart of Scotland Yard has specially requested me to go to an emergency conference in London on the problem of drug smuggling into the U.K. The doctors tell me it will be quite impossible for me to move. I am sending you.'

So it was true. Ghote's heart began thumping. To be selected to take the place of the great Superintendent Ketkar, and after only a few months under his command. He must have made more of an impression than the occasional biting remark the superintendent had addressed to him had indicated.

'Thank you, sir. Thank you,' he said.

A shimmer of puzzlement entered his scheme of things.

'But D.S.P. Jivan or D.S.P. Hiralal,' he said, mentioning the superintendent's two deputies, 'is one of them not available to go?'

The superintendent's jutting eyebrows darted together with a momentary return of his customary fire.

'Do you think I could send Jivan on a plum job like this and not send Hiralal?' he asked. 'Or send Hiralal and not Jivan? Don't be a fool, man.'

'No, sir.'

21

Glumly Ghote considered the superintendent's statement. And it was quite true. Both D.S.P. Hiralal and D.S.P. Jivan were men justly proud of their records and service. To give one the unexpected reward of a trip abroad and not the other would have been a public mortification for the unselected one which he could not have been expected to endure.

So the choice had fallen on a mere inspector. And on him in particular because he was, it came to him now, the most easily spared officer in the whole branch.

All right then. But he would do his damnedest to make a go of it away there in distant, mighty, formidable London.

'Inspector.'

Superintendent Ketkar was glaring at him and holding out a neatly clipped sheaf of paper which he had taken up from the round basket-weave table, cluttered with stacked piles of battered cardboard files, beside the high bed.

'Sir?'

'This is the text of the speech you will make to the conference. You will read it word for word as it is written.'

'Very good, sir.'

After all, that much was to be expected. What a great conference like that wanted to hear was the fruit of the immensely successful Superintendent Ketkar's experiences, not what a man three months in the branch happened to think. But all the same it would be the man three months in the branch who would actually be there, taking his rightful place among the top representatives of police forces from all over the world and making one in their proud counsels. His time would come.

'And, Inspector. You will go over my paper carefully this evening and report here at this time to-morrow to read it to me aloud.'

Ghote quailed inwardly. His voice, to put it simply, lacked the incisiveness and ready note of command which Superintendent Ketkar's all too plainly possessed. A decidedly unpleasant time lay between him and his days of triumphant exchanges of view in London.

'And one other thing, Inspector.'

'Sir?'

'You will confine yourself at the conference to answering plain questions of fact arising from my paper, and not one thing more. Understood?'

'Understood, sir.'

Ghote blinked.

The elderly-looking detective-sergeant was looking at him inquiringly, head to one side.

'Did you say something?' Ghote asked.

'I wondered whether that case was all you had in the way of baggage,' the sergeant said.

He looked down at the bulky, hideous object.

'Well, yes. Yes, it is,' Ghote replied, shamefacedly.

'Quite right, quite right,' the sergeant chirped. 'Don't want to load yourself up with a lot of useless kit.'

Ghote smiled a little.

'No, no,' he agreed.

'Just pop it in the boot of your car, shall we?'

And, before Ghote could get at the bulging case, the sergeant had seized it and was lugging it off, leaning alarmingly to one side from the weight.

Ghote would have liked to have taken it from him. After all, the sergeant – if sergeant he was – was clearly much the elder man. He looked as if he might even have been called back from retirement to help with the emergency of the conference. It was hardly right for him to be carrying such a burden, but taking it off him might start an undignified tussle. In any case it was only a few yards to the car and the driver was already getting out to help.

Ghote stood and watched as the abominable orange-brown object, looking even more hideous in colour under the light of the sodium lamps above, was finally and decently shut up in the police car's capacious luggage-compartment.

As soon as this was safely locked again, the sergeant

23

trotted round and held the back door of the car open for Ghote. Ghote dived in, gathered the folds of his enormous coat into his lap, and leant out with a parting smile.

'Thank you. Thank you, Sergeant,' he said.

The sergeant closed the door with a sharp tap.

Ghote leant back in the soothing darkness of the interior of the car. In the front seat the driver bent forward to the starting-button. The engine purred smoothly into life at his touch. Ghote relaxed against the smooth, gently smelling leather of the seat. Now things were really going with the calm efficiency which he had been led to expect, and had wondered if he would find too good to be true.

'All right, sir?' said the driver.

'Yes, certainly.'

And, like a burst of wildcat machine-gun fire, a storm of violent tapping broke out on the dark window beside his ear.

'What? What's that?'

'Think it's someone wants to speak to you, sir,' the driver said impassively.

Ghote peered into the gloom outside. Stuck hard up against the other side of the glass was the solidly plump face of Cousin Vidur.

Furiously Ghote wound down the window.

'You did not take address,' Cousin Vidur said, with open reproachfulness.

Ghote felt a pang of guilt. How much intention had he had of ever visiting them?

'I think Protima gave it to me before I left,' he said.

'All the same,' Vidur said, with a touch of authority, 'I will tell again. It is Tagore House Restaurant. You will find it in Hyde Park Terrace. That is quite close to Marble Arch. Anyone will give you directions.'

'Yes, yes,' Ghote said. 'Thank you.'

He sank back again on the leather of the seat.

But another face had joined Vidur's at the open window. It was the sergeant's.

'Anything I can do to help?' he inquired cheerfully.

Ghote sat forward again.

'This is a relative of mine,' he explained, 'distant relative. He was so kind as to meet me here. He wants me to visit him during the conference.'

But that did not satisfy Vidur. He thrust his Gandhi-capped head yet farther in at the narrow gap of the open window.

'You must come to-night,' he said urgently. 'You must come to-night, and you must stay in the house. We are depending on you. No one else but you.'

Ghote felt a hot flush of embarrassment. Were they going to be treated to another outburst about the British police?

'Very well,' he said rapidly, 'I will stay if I can.'

He turned and stared pointedly in front of him. Cousin Vidur withdrew with a final intense assessment of his good faith.

But now the sergeant thrust his tortoise neck farther in.

'If you want to cancel your hotel booking,' he said, 'I'm sure that'll be perfectly all right.'

'Oh, no. Please do not bother.'

'Well, it'd be a bit of a favour to us,' the sergeant said. 'I understand they're still looking for accommodation for one or two of the later delegates. I'll get your driver to arrange it: he'll have to take you there to collect your briefing documents.'

Ghote felt absolutely caught. He would have liked to have avoided spending all his free time in London in close contact with these cousins of his. But there seemed no way out.

'All right then,' he said, not very graciously.

The sergeant pulled his head out of the window and had a quick word with the driver. Ghote busied himself with the winding handle. And at last they were off. The driver eased the big car into gear and Ghote looked ahead of him with new interest.

But Vidur had not done. As they began to slip forward, he gave one last, echoing shout.

'Come to the back. At the back of the restaurant is the way into the house. Come to the back.'

Three

Some two hours later Ghote, setting down his atrocious suitcase beside him on a narrow brick pathway, first tapped with his bunched knuckles and then loudly knocked on the back door of the tall terraced house not far from Marble Arch to which the police car had eventually brought him.

While he waited he made up his mind once again on the exact course of action he proposed to take. He would stay with his cousins since they insisted. But he would commit himself to no active steps whatever about finding their missing niece. What he could do to convince them that the local police were the right people to handle the affair, he would do. But beyond that nothing. Absolutely nothing.

Any other course would be ridiculous. He had his work to think about. Whatever happened he was going to carry out this assignment as well as it could be carried out. He was going to be a credit to Superintendent Ketkar. That came first. And afterwards he would see as much as possible of this huge and proud city, giving in the meanwhile what comfort he could to these distant –

The door in front of him opened swiftly.

In the sharp ray of light which cut out into the darkness behind him, illuminating a jumble of high-piled, rain-slimed crates and packing-cases, he blinked dazedly. He saw that a woman dressed in a harsh red sari was standing there. Her face was in deep shadow.

'It is Mrs Datta?' he asked.

'Yes. Who is this?'

She sounded gratingly suspicious.

'It is Ganesh Ghote. Your cousin, Ganesh.'

'Ah. It is you. You have come.'

The high note of triumph was clear. Ghote redoubled his guard.

'But come in, come in, Cousin,' Mrs Datta went on. 'Do not be standing there in the darkness. Come in.'

She turned and led the way into a dingy stretch of passageway with at the end of it flights of stairs going up and down.

'Hang your coat on the pegs,' she said. 'And leave that case down here. One of the waiters will bring it up later.'

By the light of the unshaded bulb which lit the narrow back hallway, Ghote could make out that his wife's cousin was a woman of fifty or sixty, with an awkward, battling look to her, sharpened by a pair of steel-rimmed spectacles worn so close to the face that the lenses appeared to be looking out at the world from two quite differing angles. She went up the steep flight of threadbarely carpeted stairs in front of him with her elbows jutting out from side to side as if they were jabbing back at anyone or anything that dared to threaten her independence.

Ghote noted that she did not look as if she would be easily persuaded that her best course over her niece would be to let the local police carry on with their work without interference.

He sighed resignedly.

The room at the head of the stairs into which he followed Mrs Dutta came as a surprise.

He stood in the doorway blinking at it a little.

For somewhere in the heart of London, it was extraordinary Indian. More Indian by far than his own home back in Bombay. Here there was not a single chair. The bare floor was spread with some Numdah rugs and against two of the walls there were low couches covered in cheap

27

Indian printed cotton counterpanes. On the walls hung pictures of the gods in brightly coloured reproductions with garlands of artificial flowers round them. In one corner was a heavy rosewood chest, intricately carved. The whole smelt strongly of spice and aromatics.

The sole concession to the Western world, it seemed, were a popping little orange-flamed gas fire, the painted iron mantelpiece above it crammed with medicine bottles, and a battered old mahogany chest-of-drawers, its surface much cluttered with household goods, brass tumblers and tea-making apparatus including a heavy-looking gas-ring with a metal-covered pipe trailing from it down to a tap near the fire.

Mrs Datta was already at this boiling water.

'Sit, sit, Cousin,' she said. 'You will be wanting tea. You must be cold to be out on a night like this.'

Ghote noted that he was not in fact at all cold. Perhaps it was because the big dark blue police car had been well heated, or perhaps it was that the British winter was not quite so terrible as it might be.

He lowered himself cautiously down on to one of the extremely low couches and crouched on its edge a little uncomfortably.

'You have an excellent looking restaurant here,' he said experimentally.

The remark reflected something of the surprise he had felt when the police driver had set him down, by request, just outside the restaurant. It had been a great deal more luxurious than he had expected. From the few remarks Protima had made about these distant cousins of hers he had got the impression that they were struggling to make ends meet. But the Tagore House Restaurant was no poor man's enterprise. It occupied two shop fronts in a neat little row at one end of a small, quiet, decidedly prosperous street not far from the aggressively bright lights of Marble Arch and the huge blocks of flats he had glimpsed as the car had turned for a short way into Edgware Road.

The whole neighbourhood, though hardly seen, had impressed him considerably. The scrupulously bare, wide pavements, the faultlessly painted houses with their elegant black ironwork balconies and pretty illuminated fanlights over brightly coloured front doors, a small garden square protected only by a low railing yet still empty and well-kept beneath its tall, drooping, bare, elegant trees: all had proclaimed a quiet affluence that was entirely new to him.

And then had come the little row of shops – a wine merchant's, its dark window full of discreet bottles, a tobacconist's with a display of brightly opulent thick and heavy magazines, an undertaker's, remote and calm, and finally the Tagore House, two well-lit windows, deeply rich curtaining hanging down for two-thirds of their height, with in one of them a single, time-weathered bronze of the Dancing Siva and in the other, scarcely less poised, a heavily gold-framed menu card. And in the night air all round the rich aroma of fine curries.

Mrs Datta turned briefly away from her tea-making at his comment on the apparent excellence of the restaurant.

'It is an excellent restaurant,' she said.

Ghote, tired from the long, long flight and the rapid succession of new sights and sounds, found her answer totally daunting. There seemed to be no more possibly to be said.

He sat in silence.

In a few moments Mrs Datta turned away from the scratched and battered old chest-of-drawers and came towards him holding a brass tumbler of tea with the edge of her sari. Ghote took it. The metal was extremely hot and made the tips of his fingers tingle piercingly. Quickly he set it down on the floor beside him.

Mrs Datta took her own tumbler to the other couch and sat there, upright but at ease.

'Now,' she said briskly, 'what is it you are going to do to find me my peacock?'

Ghote shook his head, his tired mind grappling hard but unsuccessfully.

'Peacock?' he said.

'My husband did not tell her name?'

Ghote looked at her.

'It is my niece, Ranee,' Mrs Datta said vigorously. 'When she went to school here that is what her friends called her. It is funny to call a girl by the name of a male bird, but it is a good name for her. She is like a peacock. A fine creature, always beautiful to watch.'

Quite suddenly she got to her feet, came over and sat on the couch beside him. He saw that her hands, which had a capable and highly efficient look to them, were clutching hard at the red material of her sari.

'She was fine, fine, my Peacock,' she said. 'She had come here only half a year, and she knew everything. She could do everything. She spoke English so well, and she did well at her school too. In the school play they have made her the lead. You know what that is?'

'Yes. Yes, I know,' Ghote said.

'She was the leader of those English girls,' Mrs Datta went on. 'She was the boss of them. She knew more about things than they did, more about the ways of their own country. And she dressed always in Western clothes. You have seen the mini-skirt?'

'Not yet. But I have seen photographs in India.'

'She wore it. Not at school where it is forbidden, but after.'

Plain-faced, steel-spectacled Mrs Datta gazed into the air in front of her.

Suddenly she twisted round and laid a knobby, toil-hardened hand for an instant on Ghote's wrist.

'You must get her back, Cousin,' she said. 'You must do it.'

Ghote bent forward and felt at the top edge of the tall brass tumbler on the floor beside him. It was still very hot.

'But it would not be easy,' he said.

'But you must do it,' Mrs Datta replied, unmoved. 'You are our only chance. My husband said?'

'Yes. Yes, he said,' Ghote agreed. 'But you must remember I am here on business, important business.'

'We know it. We know. It told in the papers. It is a big conference called by Smart of the Yard. He is a very famous policeman. You will be able to ask him to help.'

Ghote's heart sank. What a situation he had got himself into, already being expected to discuss all this with a person like Detective Superintendent Smart infinitely remote from himself. How could he explain that Smart would be busy running the whole great conference with delegates drawn from the top narcotics men all over the world, and that he himself, a mere inspector, a deputy of deputies, was attending that conference by only the skin of his teeth?

He decided he would have to make a concession, a small concession. He would discuss the case a little.

'Your husband said it was three weeks since Ranee left?' he asked.

At least he could get the circumstances of the business clear in his own mind. Perhaps then some explanation would occur to him which he could use to satisfy Mrs Datta and her husband.

But Mrs Datta's reply to his tentative query led only to deeper mystery.

'Yes,' she said, 'it is three weeks. Three whole weeks since he made her go to him.'

With a feeling of hoisting aside yet another unexpected burden, Ghote put the inevitable question.

'Since he made her go to him? Who is this "he"?'

Mrs Datta set down her tumbler, which she had already succeeded in emptying, on the bare floor at her feet with a sharp tap.

'But my husband,' she said, 'he did not tell?'

'Perhaps he said something. It was very noisy at the airport. There are loudspeakers everywhere, you know.'

31

Mrs Datta drew a deep breath into her narrow jutting bosom.

'No,' she said, 'I see you have heard half only. He told that the Peacock had disappeared, yes?'

'Yes.'

'But it did not say she had been abducted?'

Ghote felt a gust of sudden fury.

'You are saying the girl has been abducted now?' he stormed. 'And who is it you are accusing? Have you informed the local police of this? I did not hear from your husband that they had taken any action in a matter such as this.'

'Oh, oh,' said Mrs Datta, 'the police have been told. But all they would say was that they were satisfied he did not do it. Satisfied. How easily they are satisfied, those policemen here.'

'But who? Who is it you are accusing?' Ghote shouted, his weariness dragging down all restraints.

'But it is Johnny Bull,' Mrs Datta said, as though here was something self-evident if every anything was.

And the name sent an abrupt streak of disquiet running through Ghote's head. It was a name he seemed to know. And it somehow meant trouble, though he could not for the life of him connect it at this moment with anything at all.

'Johnny Bull?' he said with caution.

'But, yes, Johnny Bull, the great pop singer Johnny Bull. It is he who has stolen my Peacock.'

A cold gloom descended. Nothing could be worse. Johnny Bull was a national figure, an international figure even, a singer whose name had been a household word for almost ten years. And it was him Mrs Datta was accusing of a sensational crime. There could not be anything more dangerous to get involved with just when he had his hands full, and more than full, with the Drugs Conference.

'What is it that makes you so certain he has actually abducted her?' he asked glumly.

'But she was in love with him,' Mrs Datta replied in triumph. 'In Calcutta she met him when he was making world tour. That is why she insisted to come to England. And now he has taken her. Taken away my Peacock.'

'But a man like that must have thousands of young girls who believe they are in love with him,' Ghote said desperately.

'They do not know him,' Mrs Datta replied. 'Him my Peacock knew. Well she knew him. In Calcutta and again here. In his flat she was often visitor.'

'Yes, that does make a difference, certainly,' Ghote admitted. 'But all the same you must have more evidence than that, you know.'

He picked up his tumbler of tea briskly. The brass was still good and hot but he could bear to grip it now. He took a long, careful drink.

'Evidence is it?' Mrs Datta said.

She jumped up from the couch.

'Do not think we do not have evidence. Good evidence in plenty we have.'

She marched over to the battered old mahogany chest and smartly jerked open the top left-hand drawer to its full extent. She rummaged in it briefly and brought out a square package wrapped in an old silk shawl. She placed this in a comparatively clear part of the top of the chest and began decisively unfolding it.

'You do not believe she was in love with him?' she said challengingly.

'You have told me,' Ghote answered. 'And I agree that girls often get these feelings for public figures like pop singers. It is a well-known thing.'

Mrs Datta turned away from her unwrapping and darted him a burning glance through her close-clamped steel-rimmed spectacles.

'Photos she had,' she said. 'Photos round her room of him she had, with the words of his songs under. All night she dreamt about him.'

33

A note of incongruous softness had entered her voice. Ghote realised suddenly that the Peacock's adolescent yearnings must have meant a great deal to her plain-faced, hard-working aunt. Through them she had lived in imagination a life utterly different from her own in the days of her restricted youth. No wonder she had been struck to the heart by the girl's disappearance.

He looked at her stooping back and sharply jutting elbows as she continued vigorously unwrapping her bundle.

But, no, he would not let any sympathy tug him from the decision he had made. If he was to do the work which he had come here to do properly, he could not allow himself to be distracted.

Suddenly from just outside the flimsy door of the bare room there came shatteringly an extraordinary explosion of sound. It was a voice. A man's voice. Shouting. Very, very loudly. In Bengali.

Ghote hardly spoke the language and consequently had little idea what the shouting was all about. He looked, a little bewilderedly, at Mrs Datta, who had glanced up from her bundle.

'It is my husband,' she said placidly. 'The waiters. They know nothing.'

The noise abruptly ceased, the door was thrust open and Vidur Datta came in.

A very different person, Ghote thought, from the feet-hugging weeper at the airport.

With eyes still flashing from his exercise of power down the narrow, resonating staircase outside, he looked all round the bare room. His solid little stomach jutted out now with a distinct air of command, and his head on its squat tower of neck was held at a definitely condescending angle.

'Ah, it is you, Cousin,' he greeted Ghote. 'So you have decided to come. I hope my wife has made you comfortable.'

34

'Yes, thank you, most comfortable,' Ghote answered.

He picked up the tumbler of tea again and cradled it appreciatively in his cupped hands.

'Well,' Vidur replied, 'we must look after you if you are to stay with us. It must be a stay you will enjoy.'

There was more than a trace of satisfied ownership in his voice.

'I am hoping to enjoy my time here also,' Ghote replied. 'When my duties at the conference are over, that is.'

The reminder that he was here for a purpose would not come amiss, he thought.

'Well, we shall try to do our best to make you feel you are not too far away from home,' Vidur said. 'We try to keep the West outside our doors as far as possible. As you will see.'

Ghote looked round at the irritatingly over-Indian room.

'Yes,' he said. 'Though I was hoping to be able to see something of London during my stay. There is the Tower, Big Ben, the Houses of Parliament, Buckingham Palace, New Scotland Yard.'

'If you want, if you want,' Vidur replied. 'But such things cannot match our Taj Mahal, our Jagannath Temple, our Jaipur Palace of the Winds, our painted caves at Ajanta.'

It was a rebuke, no doubt about it.

'But all the same,' Ghote said, 'when I am here there is much that it would be a shame not to see. And then I want if possible to visit the shops too. I must take back something for Protima, you know.'

He looked hard at Mrs Datta as he said this. After all, Protima was her cousin, and it was as well to let her know that he had family obligations as well as everything else.

'Yes,' she said in answer, 'there are many things in the shops. It would not take long to find something.'

Ghote seized on this opportunity, frail though it was, to

get the conversation well away from the subject of the missing Peacock.

'I would be glad of your help in this,' he said to Mrs Datta. 'I do not know what to buy. I want something that will be typical of the U.K., you know.'

To his delight, Mrs Datta put on a sharply considering look.

'It is difficult to tell,' she answered. 'I have seen some fine tea-towels with the Union Jack on them. That is very British.'

The thought horrified Ghote. That flag, symbol of a proud and glorious nation, to be used as a tea-towel.

At the risk of snubbing Mrs Datta and sending her back to her chief preoccupation, he spoke with some sharpness.

'No, no. I do not think that sort of thing at all. Something of traditional British craftsmanship.'

'But what is such craftsmanship?' Vidur Datta broke in. 'Have they anything to beat our Benares brocades, our Punjabi silverware, our Madura pottery, our Sylhet ivories, our Mirzapur carpets?'

He turned to his wife.

'Show him your blue shawl,' he said. 'Very old, but still first-rate. A first-rate job.'

Mrs Datta drew herself up.

'But I am showing,' she said. 'It is here. I am just getting out of it the letter from my Peacock.'

Caught.

'Oh, that girl and her letter,' Vidur said. 'We have had enough of her. Show Cousin Ganesh the shawl.'

But his wife's eyes, behind the slanting steel-rimmed spectacles, were flashing.

'What are you meaning?' she flamed. 'My Peacock is in the hands of this abductor, and you talk of shawls only. Cousin Ganesh is here to help us. He cannot do that until he sees the letter.'

Ghote half-expected to find himself the witness of a

36

fierce family quarrel. He felt that would be all he needed to complete his day. But disconcertingly Vidur abruptly gave way. He turned his back ostentatiously on the proceedings and tramped over to the mantelpiece where he stood examining the medicine bottles and packets ranged all along it.

His wife, an expression of active triumph on her face, finished unwrapping the shawl-enclosed bundle and took from the pile of much-handled papers that was revealed a single small sheet a little fresher than the rest.

She held it out to Ghote. He did not see how he could refuse to take it.

He read it.

'These five words only?' he asked depressedly, turning the slip over.

'It is enough,' Mrs Datta answered. 'It says she is going to Johnny Bull. Clearly it says.'

'It says "my lover",' Ghote corrected her.

'But Johnny Bull is what it means,' she said. 'Johnny Bull is the only person that can mean. And she says she is going to him. I do not read very often, but when I looked at the note straightaway I could see that.'

'And the policewoman who came, she examined it?' Ghote asked, though he knew what the answer was bound to be.

'Certainly she examined.'

'Did she ask to see anything else the Pea – anything else Ranee had written?'

It would be a neat test of the efficiency of the investigation.

'Her exercise books she saw,' Mrs Datta said proudly. 'Her exercise books she saw. Nineteen out of twenty. Nineteen out of twenty. Eighteen out of twenty. All the time. My Peacock could not have done better.'

So the policewoman had passed the test. Yet Ghote found himself unwilling to explain her efficiency to Mrs Datta. He had a feeling she would not be impressed.

37

He turned the note over again.

'Ranee did not sign?' he asked, although he could see very well that there was no signature.

'Why should she sign?' Cousin Vidur said harshly, turning away from his sulky contemplation of the top of the mantelpiece. 'Why should she sign? It was enough that she had written.'

He tapped the top of the mantelpiece with an angry little rat-tat.

'It was here,' he said. 'Here it stood, in front of the bottles. Where all could see.'

'What time was it that it was found?' Ghote asked, almost in spite of himself.

'It was the late afternoon,' Vidur replied. 'It must have been there ever since she left. But when my wife came back from her shopping – on Fridays always she goes to do the shopping, there are good Indian food shops in Drummond Street – when she came back she did not see. She does not take much notice of things written in English.'

'But you saw it when you came in here in the late afternoon?' Ghote asked.

'Yes, I saw. I read. And then I said: "So the creature has run off. That is what comes of all this Englishness. That is what comes of English friends all the time. That is what comes of English clothes".'

He marched over to Ghote.

'She wore mini-skirt,' he spluttered. 'Mini-skirt. You have seen?'

'In magazines only,' Ghote said.

'But so well she wore it.'

It was Mrs Datta. She was proclaiming her faith in the Peacock and in the Peacock's triumph over a difficult and alien way of life.

'So badly she wore,' Vidur shouted back. 'Bad. Bad. Badly. No wonder it was away she ran.'

'No. It was not so. By this man, by this Johnny Bull she has been abducted.'

She swirled round on Ghote.

38

'Cousin, you must find. You must.'

'Oh yes, find,' Cousin Vidur stormed in his turn. 'Find, find. Find or we shall have no peace in this house.'

And abruptly he wheeled round on his solidly fat little legs and pounded out of the door, slamming it behind him with a crash that seemed to shake the whole wall of the room.

Four

Mrs Datta seemed unperturbed by her husband's abrupt departure. She took the slip of paper on which the Peacock had written her curt farewell note from Ghote's fingers and carefully replaced it in the bundle of documents lying on her blue shawl.

'You must not mind my husband,' she said as she worked. 'He has gone to make *puja* only. Every night about this time he goes to the prayer-room he has made and offers *puja*. He says it is more than ever necessary in this terrible land.'

Ghote felt on the whole relieved that Vidur was no longer with them. It was going to be difficult enough making it clear that he was not going to be able to take any active part in the search for the Peacock without having two quarrelling people to contend with.

For a moment he was tempted not even to try to explain anything to Mrs Datta that night. He could say with truth that he was deadly tired. But a substratum of pride prevented him.

The instant Mrs Datta closed the drawer of the battered mahogany chest on her precious bundle he spoke.

'There is something I must say before we go any further,' he began.

Mrs Datta looked at him sharply through her skewlensed spectacles.

'You are going to tell you will not do it,' she said with quiet bitterness.

Ghote looked down at the bare floor.

'But you must understand my position,' he answered.

'I understand enough: you will not help.'

Ghote looked up.

'Please,' he said, 'if I was here for a holiday only, believe me, I would give it up at once. Even though I know there is nothing I can do. But I have work here, important work.'

Mrs Datta shook her head in sharp dismissal.

'You would have time,' she said. 'You will have time for sight-seeing, time for shopping.'

Ghote bit his lip.

'Very well then,' he said with a trace of anger, 'hear the truth. I will not get involved in this. I think you are asking for trouble, a great deal of trouble. And I will not let that sort of thing distract me from making a good job of my part in the conference.'

'Yes, that is it,' she said. 'Trouble.'

'But I cannot have my mind distracted,' Ghote said.

Mrs Datta looked up. The light from the unshaded bulb caught her spectacles.

'Trouble,' she said emphatically. 'That is what you are afraid of. Trouble. Trouble with Johnny Bull because he is a famous man. Trouble with the English because they are burra sahibs. That is what you are afraid of. I feared it even before you came.'

'No.'

Ghote felt that he would like to seize her and batter her against the drab wallpapered walls of this bare, ugly room till he had forced some sense into her.

'No,' he shouted. 'Do you think I am worried by anything of that? I am inspector of police. I have men under my command. Do you think I would let that sort of thing interfere with me if I did not want?'

40

His voice had risen to a high note of indignation. He could hear himself. He was protesting too much.

He was in fact a little afraid of this Western world. He had looked up to it for so long and from so far off that it awed him. And he knew that he ought not to let it do so.

'Yes,' Mrs Datta said in a quiet, exhausted, end-of-the-road voice. 'Yes, I see that you are afraid.'

Ghote clamped his teeth hard together.

'Very well,' he said. 'It is against my better judgment. But I will make time for your affairs. I will do it. I will do what has to be done.'

Sitting on the edge of the bed in the little room at the top of the house that had until three weeks earlier been occupied by the Dattas' niece Ranee, called the Peacock, Ghote miserably considered the events that had led up to his present situation.

How different things were on this, his first night in London, from what he had imagined they would be. The fact that he was on his way to bed in a small and dingy room in a neglected old house and surrounded by someone else's belongings did not much worry him. The prospect of life in the large Bloomsbury hotel at which he had been booked into had had complications which he was not sorry to have avoided. But he would dearly have liked not to have found himself in such an Indian atmosphere. It was not for this that he had come to modern, contemporary, yet stolidly traditional London.

But he could have put up with it. The real misery was having got himself saddled with a case, and as tricky a type of case as could be found.

He made up his mind not to do more now than just open his fearful, bulging suitcase and pull out what he would need before getting into bed.

But he did not succeed in forcing himself up. Instead he stared gloomily at the wall in front of him. It was papered in a drab shade of beige, bleached by long years of ex-

41

posure until it had reached the colour of palest coffee. Here and there it had been disfigured in various ways by the successive inhabitants of the little room. Even the Peacock, he saw, had left her mark, with a series of rectangles slightly less blanched than the surrounding areas and with rusted drawing-pins at their corners. These would be the only traces of her prized photographs of Johnny Bull, snatched down before her departure.

Determined not to let his thoughts begin to mesh with the problems these faintly dark rectangles presented, Ghote shoved himself to his feet, got his suitcase open and began making minimal preparations to go to bed.

To-morrow, or some other time, he would try to work out the meaning of the various articles the girl had abandoned all round him. Mrs Datta had apologised about them when she had shown him up to the room – the bright dresses drooping bedraggledly in the cheap wardrobe, the froth of nylon underwear in the drawers of the dressing-table, and the collection of cheap-looking, three-parts-used cosmetics on its top, pushed by some tidying hand into a single solid clump.

But now he had to get to bed and sleep. If he was to conduct himself well next day at the conference, he must not let his thoughts get on to the racing treadmill they were all too ready to send whirling interminably round far into the night.

He slumped down on the edge of the bed ready to swing himself in. And his bare toes came into contact with something that had been hidden by the cotton counterpane. He looked down.

Beside his foot was one of a pair of Indian-made *chappals*, the imprint of the toes of the girl who had owned them worn deep into the old, much-used, glistening dark leather.

The discarded object spoke to him, clearly and with inescapable simplicity, of the girl whose foot had made those marks on the stained sole. All the newly-bought, cheapish underwear and the jostling, frilly mass-produced dresses had told him only that his case was concerned with an empty-headed teenager, one like thousands of others, in Bombay, in Calcutta, in London, anywhere in any of the big cities of the world. But the old *chappal* had belonged to one distinct person, the Peacock. It was pitifully imprinted with her mark.

Girls of her age grew up fast. The day three weeks ago when she had abandoned this relic of her past life she had been almost a woman, sophisticated and knowing. The day when this *chappal* had been bought for her, two or three years before, she had been a child. Her whole history was in the grooved and stained leather. The rapid development on the hardly secure base, the suppressed anxieties and fears, the bold front and the still childish creature beneath.

Ganesh Ghote stood up in the little room at the top of the old house and made a resolution. If there was one small thing he could do to find this girl and bring her back to her rightful place, to this room, to this narrow bed, he would do it.

He got into the bed, humped the blankets over his exposed shoulder and fell deeply asleep.

But from the moment Ghote awoke next morning, feeling much more capable of dealing with the onrush of events after nine hours of heavy sleep, he realised that for all the vividness of the image of the missing Peacock that had risen up in front of him the night before, he was going to have to put the whole business of her disappearance right to the back of his mind. The Conference on the Smuggling of Dangerous Drugs overwhelmingly filled the foreground.

He knew from his briefing papers that the opening session of the conference was to take place at 10 a.m. in a hall at Wood Street police-station off Cheapside in the City. He decided to leave Tagore House in plenty of time.

43

Unless he had ample opportunity to spy out the lie of the land, he knew he would not be happy. The prospect of pushing forward to ask about things he could possibly be expected to know for himself was one he was not going to submit to if he could help it.

So, after an ample breakfast, not of the sausages, tea and toast he had fondly imagined he would have on this morning, but of well fried rice and Mrs Datta's carefully prepared pickles, he heaved his enormous English-style coat off its peg, plunged his way into it and set out.

He followed his cousins' directions carefully to the nearest Underground station, Marble Arch, and there, to supplement the instructions in his briefing, he bought himself a guide to London. Even handing over two such extremely English coins as the couple of half-crowns he parted with for this was, he found, a positive pleasure. And now he felt really well equipped. He could go here and there in this great city with the minimum need to show himself an ignoramus by having to ask for help at every turn.

Cautiously he made his way down to the Tube plat-form. The train, when he got into it, was immensely crowded, but the mass of people seemed infinitely more orderly than those of the similar morning rush in Bombay. Even in the very closest proximity they contrived to ignore each other with magnificent calm. He felt proud of them.

It was at about this time that he became fully aware of his first live mini-skirt. In the preoccupation of making sure he got on the right train going in the right direction he had had eyes for nothing but illuminated notices. Then he had been too jammed tight to see anything. But now as the train cleared a little, he found himself looking straight down the long carriage at two girls with skirts showing four long plump stretches of nylon-covered leg above four soft rounded knees.

For perhaps two minutes he regarded the phenomenon

44

earnestly. Then he found that his mind was made up. He did not approve.

But already the station names were getting dangerously near to the ones immediately before the Bank, where his briefing had told him to alight. He concentrated his full attention on being absolutely ready to jump from the train the moment it reached his destination.

He made it with colours flying.

He negotiated the tricky circular exit from the station without a hitch. Out in the street, he paused long enough to be absolutely sure he had got his bearings and then set off following the directions in his briefing, happily confident that he was not putting a single foot wrong.

He found each turning exactly where he expected it to appear. He noted with a comforting feeling that the walk from the Tube to Wood Street was taking not a moment longer than he had thought likely. He spotted the tall, strikingly modern building that he guessed would be the newly-built model police-station which the briefing had described well before he got to it. And when he arrived at the broad flight of entrance steps, sure enough they proved to be those of the building itself.

The only trouble was that he had arrived one hour and twenty-seven minutes too early.

Ghote walked hastily round the corner so that no one coming out of the building should spot him as a conference delegate who had made the mistake of turning up so ridiculously long before necessary. And there he stood and considered.

He felt annoyed with himself, not so much at the ridiculousness of his early arrival, which had its funny side, but because of all the things he could have done with a full hour to spare towards fulfilling the promise he had made himself the night before about the missing Peacock.

He could have gone over some of the clothes and personal possessions she had left behind. Although no doubt

45

the policewoman who had visited the Tagore House would have checked, there still might be something to find. Experience counted in such matters. Or he could have paid a call on the local police-station. That would be an essential preliminary.

But now the time was simply going to waste.

He looked round at the hurrying crowds of office workers and at the sedate but impressive buildings on all sides, quietly contriving to make it clear that they occupied an inner centre of the commercial undertakings of all the wide world.

It was certainly something, he reflected, even to be standing where he was. And then a notion flitted into his head.

For a minute or two he pored over the pages of his paper-covered guide. And, yes, he should be able to do it. From where he was standing it could not be more than fifteen minutes' walk to the Tower of London.

He would go now, and see with his own eyes those hallowed stones where Queens had knelt at the block and Kings had died at the hands of murderers. All that he had been told as a boy, when Anglo-Indian Mr Merrywether, his teacher of long ago, had hammered out to a cowed, attentive class the facts of the glorious and ancient history of England, would come suddenly to life.

He set off at a brisk pace, along the street called London Wall, along Wormwood Street, across Bishopsgate, along Houndsditch. The very names were deeply evocative of the crowded, tumultuous past. They sang to him of proud City liverymen, of time-honoured traditions. And the intent, jostling passers-by spoke of the vigorous pursuit of the business of to-day, still carried on in these same greyly dignified streets.

Only the sight of a middle-aged shop assistant, long-faced and lugubrious in a grey overall reaching to below his knees, sweeping steadily and methodically at the floor of an ironmonger's, made him pause momentarily. At home the sight would have been almost impossible. There sweepers swept and shop assistants held fast to their ordained task of serving customers with due and proper ceremony. Did this man find his broom shameful? He looked mournful, but hardly ashamed. If this was the custom, he must be used to it.

He hurried on. And then, as he climbed a slight ascent going along the oddly-named Minories, he saw it – the Tower. Its outline was unmistakable. He had looked at it a thousand times in advertisements, in newspaper articles, on calendars. And beyond it was Tower Bridge, the one that could be raised to let ships pass. And there must be the mighty Thames itself.

For a second he was surprised, shocked almost. The water of the great river was not, as it had been on a hundred brightly coloured maps, a crisp and inviting blue. It was instead plainly a dirty brown, indistinguishable by and large from the familiar dirty waters of Bombay Harbour. But soon, as he looked a little longer at the broad river sweeping by, he was able to reassure himself that it was indeed a truly incontrovertibly majestic sight.

He made his way round the wide emptied moat of the dark-walled Tower looking for the public entrance.

How green the grass was in that huge ditch once filled with water to protect the ancient fighting-men who had guarded the old City from their grim bastion above him. And how ordered and dignified now were the people of this latter age as they streamed past this great monument of the past on their way to the demanding and complex tasks of to-day.

Even when at the sober blue-painted ticket offices he discovered that the building did not open to the public till ten o'clock his enthusiasm was not diminished. He crossed the broad street, sat down on a bench in the little public garden opposite and drew in a long breath of admiration.

There it all was before him, like a gigantic and succulent

meal waiting to be devoured. And it would wait. It would still be there, its ancient history-soaked stones unviolated, whenever he chose to come back and take his fill of them. The grim old building seemed at that moment to hold for him in one graspable whole all the past centuries of this noble, sea-girt isle.

The huge black and grey walls rose up massively in front of him. Beyond them the pinnacled inner towers stood out against the softly grey sky. Which one of them was the Bloody Tower, he wondered. Never mind. When he made his proper visit he would find out for certain and savour its rich associations to the utmost.

For a brief moment he caught a glimpse on a high inner gallery of a Beefeater, a sudden richly coloured figure lighting up the sombreness all around. And, he thought, in due time he would see such figures by the dozen. And the ancient ravens that haunted the place. And the very axe under which Queens had bowed their necks. And the glowing splendour of the Crown Jewels, symbols of the proud and ancient monarchy of this proud and ancient land.

He gazed and gazed.

Yet, oddly enough, at the very moment when he got up to go back to Wood Street police-station, leaving himself a decently reasonable amount of time for the return walk, he found suddenly that he was overwhelmed almost to drowning point, it seemed, by a totally unexpected and desperately acute attack of home-sickness.

It was stupid, but abruptly he wanted to be back in India. He wanted the brightness, the noise, the easy-goingness. He wanted, he found to his simple astonishment, to be standing looking at peacocks.

Peacocks. Nothing else. He wanted to see the gaudy plumage, the bright, light-reflecting jewel colours of the proud birds.

He shook his head angrily.

What nonsense was this? It was obviously connected with the extraordinary name Mrs Datta used for her niece. But it was absurd to be thinking of peacocks now, thinking of peacocks strolling in the wide terraced gardens of the great Bombay houses up on Malabar Hill, when at this moment he was in the heart of London. Here he was truly and actually treading the streets of the great city he had wanted to see ever since he was a boy, and had never imagined he would even get near to, and he could do nothing better than think about a lot of tawdry birds.

He squared his shoulders under the loose mantle of his huge checked coat and tramped stern-faced off towards Wood Street.

There he found that all was ready for the conference. An extremely polite, short-haired, eager police-cadet showed him where to hang his coat and led him along to the hall where the conference itself was to take place.

It was a spacious, high-ceilinged, extremely imposing room, very modern-looking but not neglecting the traditional. All the way down either side were tall windows set in deep wooden frames, standing impressively out against the white of the walls. At each end huge curtains dropped from ceiling to floor in a great dignified sweep of deep rust colour. At the top was a shallow platform with a single table on it and a few chairs. Facing this rows of other chairs were ranged, elegant and glossy in black leather.

Behind these there was a clear space where the first arrivals were standing, mostly chatting with each other. More delegates were being shown in at every moment.

Ghote knew that, for the honour of the Indian police, he ought to go up to one of the people standing there and make good conversation. But somehow he kept putting the moment off.

He noticed a smiling, busily talking Japanese whose confident English gave him a considerable qualm. There were several broad-shouldered, attentively polite Americans. There were various Europeans whom he could not precisely place, and there was a tall, bearded Pakistani.

Surely he could talk to him about something. He made

49

up his mind to dart forward. But at that very instant the Pakistani was eagerly buttonholed by one of the European delegates, evidently an old acquaintance, and Ghote felt it would be impolite to barge in.

Then over at the far side of the hall he caught a glimpse of his sergeant friend of the evening before. Here was someone it would be quite easy to go over and talk with, to thank him for his help at the airport. But was this just taking the easy way out? It would be hiding under the skirts of one of the organising staff when he ought to be engaging as an equal with the other delegates. He stayed put.

The minutes went by.

Then abruptly he was seized with a fury against himself. If this was the best he could do, he ought to go back to the Tagore House and do something about finding out what had happened to that poor girl.

He straightened his back and marched across to the nearest disengaged figure, a somewhat dapper man with large rimless glasses set squarely across a puggish nose.

'Good morning,' he said, 'may I introduce myself? Inspector Ghote, Bombay, representing India.'

The words sent a shiver of pride through him as he pronounced them.

The dapper man with the rimless glasses bowed slightly and smiled.

'Commissaris Goedhuis, Netherlands Police.'

They shook hands with great heartiness.

'Well,' Commissaris Goedhuis said, 'do you find it altogether too cold for you here?'

It was an innocent and friendly enough question. But it almost undid Ghote. Because he realised suddenly that he had not felt it in the least cold, that he had even unconsciously opened the buttons of his huge overcoat as he had hurried back to the conference. And this was England in November.

Luckily, he had hardly begun to stammer out an answer when there came a sharp burst of extremely martial music from two big loudspeakers at the back of the hall. Everybody looked up. The music stopped in mid-phrase as abruptly as it had started. There was some mystified laughter, during which a man in uniform rapped sharply on the table up on the shallow stage.

'Gentlemen,' he said, 'if you will be so good as to be seated, the Commissioner of the City of London Police will say a few words.'

Everybody moved to the precisely arranged rows of black leather chairs. The commissioner stood. He hoisted up the microphone in front of him. From the loudspeakers came a protesting grinding noise. There was a hush. The conference had begun.

Ghote listened with close attention to the commissioner's speech of welcome, but after a little he felt relaxed enough to give some attention to the little group seated up on the platform. They were presumably the morning's various speakers. With a tightening feeling in his stomach, he realised that the time would come when he himself would sit in one of their places with Superintendent Ketkar's prepared paper in his hand. He tried to remember the exact emphases the superintendent had indicated he wanted made at certain key points. He felt hot. Only the sight of his elderly sergeant friend of the night before sitting all by himself at the edge of the platform did something to reassure him. If someone like that could take a place up there, no doubt with some organisational duties, then he in his turn could surely sit at ease under the scrutiny of his fellow delegates.

The commissioner began bringing his speech to a conclusion.

'And now,' he said, 'I have only one duty remaining, a most pleasant one. And that is to introduce to you, as convener of this conference, a person known by repute, I

51

am sure to all of you, Detective Superintendent Smart of the Metropolitan Force.'

There was a solid pattering of applause. The commissioner sat down. And from the side of the platform there walked modestly forward the elderly detective-sergeant.

Five

Ghote sat there on his smart black leather chair and wished that the glossy parquet floor of the loftily imposing hall would open up and swallow him completely. Or that one of the glass crystal globes of the impressive hanging lights would crash instantly down on to his offending head.

How could he have done it? He had actually called him 'Sergeant' to his face. He had leant out of the car and said 'Thank you, Sergeant.' To Detective Superintendent Smart, Smart of the Yard, one of the leading police authorities on dangerous drugs in the world, and a particular friend of his own Superintendent Ketkar.

He sat stunned.

And meanwhile up on the platform Smart himself was modestly and simply outlining the main plan of the conference. Ghote hardly heard a word. How totally unassuming the great man was, he thought dazedly. Look at the way he had simply picked up that abominable suitcase and lugged it to the car. A full-blown superintendent doing that for a mere inspector and a much younger man. Really it would have been impossible to tell he was a person held in the highest regard all over the world. What simplicity, what modesty. How utterly British.

Even when Smart sat down, to sustained applause from every part of the hall, Ghote still remained bemused by the enormity of the mistake he had made. How would he ever face him when they met again, as in the close-knit group of the conference they must?

He paid no attention at all to the delegate who stood up to deliver the first paper of the conference. It was more than half over before he realised that he had failed to take a single note. He snatched up his brand-new notebook and flicked it wildly open.

It was the one thing he had promised himself: he would deliver back to Superintendent Ketkar a full and complete account of every word that had been said at the conference. And already that ambition was incapable of fulfilment.

Desperately he began to scribble.

So it was in a mood of angry determination that Ghote arrived back at the Tagore House after his first day at the Smuggling of Drugs Conference. His prompt failure to reach the ideal he had set himself for his conduct there was rubbing at his mind, he felt, like the knobby shaft of a bullock-cart might rub at a sore on an animal's flank. But it made him all the more resolved to conquer this other task that had been thrust upon him.

With the key to the back door which Mrs Datta had given him that morning, he let himself quietly in, hung his vivid green-and-yellow coat on its hook, and went quickly up to the top of the house without attempting to see host or hostess.

He would start straightaway by making the thorough check he had promised himself on every item the Peacock had left behind her. Later, if there was time, he would get in contact with the local police and find out precisely what inquiries they had already made.

A programme lay ahead.

He was not to get far with it. Scarcely had he opened the cheap, old wardrobe and turned a fresh page at the back of his notebook when a sharp knock sounded on the door behind him.

He turned round. The door was already open and Mrs

Datta was standing there.

'Well, Cousin,' she said, 'you are back.'

'Yes. Yes, I am back,' Ghote said.

He waited to be asked how his day had gone. He would make some not too precise reply, he decided.

'If you wish to eat before you go,' Mrs Datta said, 'I will tell them down in the kitchens to serve a meal at once.'

'Go?' said Ghote.

'To Johnny Bull.'

Ghote felt a flood of hot rage. Damn it all, he was doing what the wretched woman wanted. Against his better judgment, he had undertaken to set to work tracking down the missing Peacock. He even wanted to find her, to restore her to her proper home. And the obstinate she-devil was telling him how he ought to set about it, ordering him off to see this Johnny Bull before he had even begun to get his bearings in the case.

And, down below the flood-tide of his rage, there lurked the uneasy thought that he did not in truth in the least want to go and see the famous Johnny Bull.

'At present I am conducting a search of the girl's remaining possessions,' he said with iron calm.

'But they are what she has left behind only,' Mrs Datta replied.

'I think you do not understand. What a missing person has left behind often provides most valuable indications to their present whereabouts.'

'She is with Johnny Bull. Everybody knows.'

Ghote sighed.

'If that was certain,' he said, 'the local police would have taken action against Mr Bull. But the note the Peacock left did not mention him by name. The girl may have had some other person she called her lover.'

Mrs Datta shook her head in total negative.

'She did not.'

'But how can you be so sure?'

'To me she told everything.'

The long, ugly face with its squashed-on spectacles and its jutting unlovely jaw looked back at him in serene triumph.

Ghote saw that, whatever the actual truth, she was not going to be convinced easily that the bright, gay creature through whom she had lived her missed youth could possibly not have given to her her total confidence.

Yet he made the attempt.

'Come,' he said sharply, 'young girls do not tell everything to older people. That is well known.'

Mrs Datta drew herself up like a tiger.

'But I am not the girl's mother,' she retorted. 'To a mother a girl is afraid of speaking, yes. But to a favourite aunt, to one who understands, she tells everything.'

But the look of overpowering confidence had seeped away. A strain showed in the set of the ugly, heavy, jutting jaw.

'Do you think,' she demanded abruptly, 'that to those silly giggling girls she told the truth? Her friends they were. Oh, yes. But she was the leader of them. To them she would not tell everything. No.'

A glimmer of an idea entered Ghote's head.

'These friends,' he said cautiously, 'what are their names?'

But Mrs Datta was not so easily to be caught.

'Is it to them you are thinking of going?' she replied. 'Oh, yes, you would not find them difficult to talk. Talk they will and plenty, if it is idle nonsense you want to hear. But it is to Johnny Bull that you should be going. To him only.'

Ghote made a concession.

'No doubt it will be necessary to interview Mr Johnny Bull before too long,' he said. 'But first it is necessary to make a thorough examination here.'

Mrs Datta shrugged her bony shoulders under the glaring green sari she was wearing this evening.

'That woman policeman came in here,' she said. 'At all

my Peacock's things she looked. For half an hour she was here.'

Ghote smiled.

'Then shall we see what two or three hours' really thorough investigation will do?' he said.

'And all that time this Johnny Bull has my girl in his hands.'

She stared at him implacably.

He said nothing. But at the bottom of his mind he nurtured a small, hard gem of determination. He was not going to be pushed into seeing Johnny Bull one moment before he was ready.

He looked at the gaping door of the cheap wardrobe and at the close packed row of bright cotton dresses, skirts and blouses. What he ought to do was calmly to continue inspecting them, taking out each garment in turn, methodically examining it, entering its description in his notebook and replacing it.

But the thought of doing all this to an accompaniment of Mrs Datta persistently telling him it was time he went to see Johnny Bull was more than he could face.

A compromise came to him.

He turned to Mrs Datta.

'Perhaps on second thoughts,' he said, 'this would be the most convenient time to visit the local police and hear from them full details of the matter.'

'But what is it you will hear?' Mrs Datta replied contemptuously. 'That they are satisfied that Johnny Bull is the best of men only.'

'It may turn out that they have not been able to make all the inquiries they would have wished,' Ghote said mildly. 'I know all the police here are considerably below establishment. No doubt that accounts for the short time the policewoman spent examining these clothes.'

'But if they were not properly thorough, you should go at once to Johnny Bull,' Mrs Datta replied.

The glimmer of logic in her reply touched off Ghote's fury once more.

'I am going to the police-station,' he snapped.

'It is to Johnny Bull you should go.'

'Will you kindly inform which police-station it is that you went to?'

'Johnny Bull's address I know well. Often my Peacock told me it. It is Suite B, Carlton Tower, S.W.1.'

'Thank you,' Ghote said, with swingeing irony, 'that will be most useful in due course. And now the address of the police-station?'

'You will not be needing.'

Ghote retained his calm.

'Very well,' he replied, 'I will go and find your husband. I am sure he will be good enough to tell me.'

Mrs Datta produced, in face of this, an equal calm.

'My husband is making *puja*. He is never allowed to be disturbed.'

'Then perhaps you will tell me yourself?'

'The Carlton Tower is in Sloane Street. You can go by Number 137 bus.'

Ghote assumed a tone of greatly wondering surprise.

'You do not wish to tell me where is the police-station?'

'You do not need to know.'

'I consider that I do. And I shall make the request to your husband, wherever he is.'

Ghote had noticed on his way up the threadbare stairs that the door of Cousin Vidur's prayer-room, open wide in the morning, had been firmly shut. He had felt relieved. There was something decidedly daunting in the prospect of being asked to join his host in the almost completely bare room with its solitary picture of Sri Ramakrishna surrounded by a garland of dusty dried flowers with only a flimsy-looking card-table set in front of it bearing a few saucers of strong-smelling incense and offerings.

But, however sacrosanct to the master of the house the room was, the gem of hard determination at the bottom of his mind was glowing too fiercely now to be checked.

He marched across the Peacock's little bedroom.

'I am going down now,' he said, giving Mrs Datta a hard look almost nose-to-nose.

She said nothing.

He went past her out of the door. He was conscious of the fact that Vidur Datta, the tyrant of the home, would be an awkward person to beard in his holy of holies.

At a dignified pace he set off down the narrow, grimly carpeted stairs. Mrs Datta moved to the small landing outside the Peacock's room and watched him.

He reached the foot of the first flight of stairs. As he turned to go down the next flight, he forced himself not to look back up.

And then through the half-open door of the living-room immediately in front of him he heard a curious noise. It was a deep, burbling humming-sound.

In a moment he realised what it was. Rapidly he completed his descent of the stairs and entered the over-Indian room.

There, standing by the bottle-crowded mantelpiece with the little orange gas fire popping merrily away beneath, was Vidur Datta. His face wore an expression of benign cheerfulness and he was humming away at his little song in a deep baritone voice.

'Good evening, Cousin,' Ghote said.

'Ah, Cousin, it is you. Good. Good.'

Prayer had apparently mellowed him. Ghote struck while the iron was hot.

'I am thinking of calling to see the police here,' he said. 'To find out exactly what they have done about your niece, you know.'

Vidur looked at him solemnly.

'An excellent plan,' he replied. 'Excellent. Not that you will learn anything. They had no interest in the matter. But you must see for yourself.'

So, keeping a wary eye on the door in case Mrs Datta made a sudden rush down, Ghote asked casually which police-station it was that he should go to. And Vidur immediately gave him the address.

He even went to the length of writing it carefully down for him, clearing away some of the bottles on the mantelpiece to do so. Ghote came and stood beside him.

He saw with some awe that every single one of the medicines ranged there was a laxative.

But, for all the ease with which obstacles had been overcome, Ghote did not find, when he entered the police-station some thirty minutes later, that his troubles were over.

He walked into the old-fashioned, much-scrubbed, high-ceilinged room across which ran a broad, dented, notched and shiny public counter with a fair degree of confidence. This might be unknown, awe-inspiring London, but it was also familiar territory.

But the solitary occupant of the room, a sergeant on the far side of the counter, sitting at a large, cluttered table, typing away with two battering fingers at an aged, clack-etty machine, simply gave him the briefest of glances and returned to his work.

Ghote waited for a little. But nothing happened. So he coughed. But still nothing happened. At last, with a disconcerting feeling that things were not going to go to plan, he rapped loudly on the shiny top of the counter.

The broad-backed sergeant turned slowly round. Ghote saw that he had a long, florid face and that his teeth, which sprawled out of his mouth in every direction, were as yellow as a horse's.

He got up, swung his way heavily across and leant on the counter opposite Ghote.

'Yes?' he said. 'Sir?'

Ghote could not help thinking that this was not his image of the true British police-sergeant. But appearances could be deceiving.

'Good evening,' he said politely.

The sergeant, leaning on his elbows, said nothing.

Ghote drew a long breath.

'It is rather an awkward matter,' he ventured.

59

The sergeant shot him a look under tangled hairy eyebrows.

'Girl, is it? Got her into trouble, have you?'

'No, no, no, no. It is nothing like that.'

The sergeant did not look as if he believed this.

Ghote frowned at himself and began again.

'I am as a matter of fact a police officer also.'

'Oh, yes?'

The sergeant took his elbows off the battered counter and stood back the more easily to give Ghote a look radiating pure disbelief.

He seemed to Ghote a far cry from the blue-uniformed figure which he had observed with feelings of almost holy joy at London Airport some twenty-four hours before. The conclusion was inescapable.

He plunged his hand into the heavy depths of his overcoat.

'Look,' he said, 'let me show you.'

He made contact with his passport, pulled it out and opened it on the counter.

The sergeant gave it a glance.

'Inspector, eh?' he said without enthusiasm. 'Bombay police.'

'I am here for the Conference on the Smuggling of Dangerous Drugs,' Ghote said. 'And as a matter of fact I am staying with some distant relations of my wife's.'

'Oh, yes? Very nice.'

'It is not.'

The thought of how far from nice it was stung Ghote to a sharpness he had not dreamt of producing in these surroundings. The sergeant now looked at him with genuine curiosity.

'It is not nice,' Ghote went on firmly. 'It is extremely unpleasant for me because three weeks ago a young girl disappeared from the house.'

The sergeant sighed. He turned back to the table and picked up a big leather-bound register.

'Name?' he said.

Inwardly Ghote groaned. The whole business seemed doomed to a series of misunderstandings.

'The matter has already been reported,' he said.

The sergeant banged the register closed.

'However,' Ghote said, stung into acidity again, 'my relatives are by no means happy with the action taken by your department.'

Silently the sergeant lowered his elbows on to the counter directly in front of Ghote. He leant towards him.

'Not happy?' he said menacingly.

But such blatant opposition, even from someone he had been prepared to honour, could have only one effect on Ghote.

'No, they are not happy,' he said, with considerable sharpness now. 'And I have come to satisfy myself that in fact the fullest inquiries have been made.'

The sergeant stood up, looking offended to the very last of his sprawling yellow teeth.

'I think you can trust us to carry out our own business, sir.'

'I hope so,' Ghote replied remorselessly. 'But I must still ask to see the woman police constable who came to the house.'

'That depends on whether she's available,' the sergeant said.

Ghote looked at him steadily.

'I have preferred to come here myself,' he said, 'rather than put the matter in the hands of my colleague at the conference, Detective Superintendent Smart.'

The sergeant's mouth shut like a trap over his sprawling teeth.

'What date did this alleged offence occur upon, sir?' he said grumpily.

'Upon October the twenty-first last.'

With maddening deliberation, the sergeant undid the silver button on the chest pocket of his uniform. He pulled out a clumsy-looking bright red diary and began flicking through its pages, occasionally pausing to lick his thumb.

'Ah,' he said at last, 'Oct, twenty one. Trafalgar Day. It'll be W.P.C. Mackintosh you'll be wanting.'

'Please,' said Ghote, still implacable.

'I'll see if she's in,' the sergeant said.

He turned and lumbered across the room to a tall, well-scrubbed door.

Ghote waited.

Trafalgar Day, he thought. He saw the proud British men-o'-war, which Anglo-Indian Mr Merrywether had once described in such glowing terms, using his cane with a zeal well above and beyond the line of duty when anyone appeared not to be paying the closest attention. The tall ships came crowding down on the might of Napoleon's navy, their cannon raking the Frenchmen from stem to stern. 'England Expects Every Man To Do His Duty.' There had been a brightly coloured print of H.M.S. *Victory* flying this signal in the school corridor, inviting long hours painstakingly translating the code of its gay little flags.

It would be on that day of all days that the Peacock had chosen to cut and run.

The well-scrubbed door opened and the sergeant came in followed by a tall policewoman wearing her smart uniform with dash.

Ghote saw at once that she was the ideal English Rose come to life. Under her blue peaked cap her hair was crisply golden. Her complexion was a vigorous pink and white. She held herself trimly and her eyes were the brightest blue.

'This is him,' the sergeant said to her.

He jerked his head in Ghote's direction, went over to the cluttered table and busied himself battering away once more at the keys of the old typewriter.

The English Rose came over to Ghote.

'Do I understand you wish to make a complaint?' she said, with unmistakable cold hostility.

62

'No, no,' Ghote answered hastily. 'No complaint. Perhaps the sergeant told you the circumstances?'

'You're staying at a place where a girl went missing and I made some inquiries,' Policewoman Mackintosh said.

She made it sound as if Ghote was about to accuse her of criminal activities of the worst sort.

'It was at the Tagore House Restaurant,' he said.

'I remember the case.'

Her blue, blue eyes were icily challenging.

'Please do not think that I am in any way accusing you in this matter,' Ghote said. 'I would simply be most grateful for any information you have.'

But the blue eyes stayed sapphire-hard.

'Any information was passed back to the original informants,' she intoned.

'I know. I know. But my relatives expect me to do something.'

'Well, there's nothing you can do,' the English Rose said tersely. 'The girl's gone off with some boy-friend or other and they just won't believe it. I remember the details: it's as clear a case as you'll get.'

She turned away, smartly as a soldier on parade. Her squared shoulders and the crisp line of golden curls under her cap all said one thing: that's the way to treat fussing foreigners, be absolutely firm.

Ghote saw that if he was going to get anything out of her he had to act fast.

'Oh, yes,' he said, in as hearty, rollicking, man-to-man tone as he could contrive. 'Came to the same conclusion myself as soon as I had time to look about a bit. I can see you size up a case pretty damn' quickly.'

And, a little to his surprise, the blatant flattery worked. Policewoman Mackintosh turned round again. Her blue eyes were beginning to glint with pleasure.

'You get a feel for these things,' she said.

Ghote leant on the counter with comradely carelessness.

'Not every one does,' he said. 'Believe you me.'

Policewoman Mackintosh actually smiled.

'Well, perhaps not.'

'No,' Ghote said, 'I dare say you see what my trouble is now?'

Policewoman Mackintosh gave him a sympathetic grin.

'Yes,' he said, 'it is a question of bloody well convincing the old people that what we know happened has happened.'

'Yes,' said Policewoman Mackintosh thoughtfully, 'you've got a problem there all right.'

She stood pondering. Ghote adopted a face of rueful despair.

'Tell you what,' she said after a little, 'you could try 'em with the old A4 Index.'

'The A4 Index? We do not use anything called that in Bombay.'

'No, it's a thing they run at the Yard. Pretty useful at times. It's a list of any girl under twenty-one who's ever come to the notice of the police. Doesn't matter whether she's got a conviction, just if she's come to our notice.'

'And this girl Ranee, the Peacock as they call her, she was on it?'

Policewoman Mackintosh gave a sudden sort of a laugh.

'The Peacock,' she said. 'That's right. I went and saw a couple of her friends from school and they called her that. What a name.'

'You saw her friends?' Ghote asked with some eagerness. 'Did you learn anything from them?'

'Well,' Policewoman Mackintosh said, leaning in a friendly way on the other side of the broad, pock-marked counter, 'I thought I'd better do a bit of checking up. It's always tricky knowing how much truth you're being told dealing with foreigners.'

She registered Ghote's brown face not a yard from her own.

'If you don't mind my saying so,' she added.

'Not at all, not at all,' Ghote answered. 'I have the same problem myself with Englishmen in Bombay.'

'Oh. Yes. I suppose so.'

Policewoman Mackintosh looked thoughtful.

'But did you find anything useful from those girls?' Ghote said.

A look of frank disgust appeared on Policewoman Mackintosh's pink-and-white features.

'Not a thing,' she said. 'A silly, cheeky pair of giggling nits if ever I saw any.'

Her blue eyes sparked cold fire.

The way her encounter with the Peacock's two friends had gone became startlingly clear to Ghote. There had been misunderstandings on both sides.

And with the vision of this there came an exciting thought. It was plain from the bitterness Mrs Datta had shown in speaking about the Peacock's schoolfriends that the girl had indeed confided in them more than a little. And, equally, it was clear that Policewoman Mackintosh had not been told about these confidences. Yet, if anyone knew what had been in the Peacock's mind before she vanished, it would be these two.

'Tell me – ' he began cautiously.

But suddenly from the splay-teethed sergeant down at the cluttered, untidy table there came a deep guffaw of laughter.

'Suppose you got a bit more out of that Johnny Bull feller, Mackintosh,' he said. 'A hell of a lot more.'

Policewoman Mackintosh's sturdy pink and-white complexion turned a shade pinker.

'I went there with D.S. Turner,' she said tersely.

'To Johnny Bull's?' Ghote said. 'I would be most interested to hear your conclusions. Was that a detective-sergeant you saw him with?'

'Yes. Thought two heads would be better than one dealing with someone well-known like that,' Policewoman Mackintosh replied.

She sounded distinctly grateful for Ghote's quick intervention.

'Well,' she went on, 'we found Johnny Bull accounted for his movements on the night in question pretty well.'

'Oh, yes?' said Ghote. 'How was that?'

Policewoman Mackintosh gave a short laugh.

'Had girl-friend with him,' she said. 'A little blonde, name of Sandra. She was there when we called, and she was there on October the twenty-first. In fact, I got the impression she never lets the great Johnny out of her sight.'

'I see,' said Ghote. 'And a person like that would hardly be likely to tolerate the presence of another female.'

Policewoman Mackintosh grinned broadly.

'You size up a situation pretty quickly yourself,' she said.

Ghote grinned back. Then he looked suddenly depressed.

'So it looks as if there will not be a lot to tell them at the Tagore House,' he said.

'Well, I dare say she'll turn up soon enough,' Policewoman Mackintosh replied sympathetically. 'You know what girls of that age are like over boy-friends sometimes.'

Once more the yellow-toothed sergeant found a comment.

''Ark at her,' he said. 'W.P.C. Mackintosh, butter wouldn't melt in her mouth. I bet you give your boy-friends something to think about all the same, eh?'

'Well, thank you, Miss Mackintosh,' Ghote said loudly. 'You have been more than helpful.'

'Not at all. Sorry there wasn't more I could do.'

Ghote, turning away from the counter, paused.

'Perhaps there is one thing,' he said. 'If I could have the names and addresses of those friends of the Peacock's, then if Mrs Datta continues to be anxious I can go and see them.'

At the old typewriter, the sergeant looked up. His long higgledy-piggledy yellow teeth glinted.

'I don't think we can do that there 'ere,' he said. 'What you might call confidential information, that is.'

Policewoman Mackintosh gave him a sharp look.

'But we're going to make an exception for a distinguished visiting police officer,' she said.

Six

Ghote left the police-station with feelings of considerable satisfaction. He had at least hit on a line of inquiry which had not yet been pursued. He made up his mind to follow it to the very end.

Buried deep in his enormous check coat, he plunged through the misty evening not uncontent with the way things were now going.

In the neat, well-kept square near the restaurant the bare forms of the elegantly drooping trees stood out by the light of the tall street-lamps a deeper black against the faint whiteness of the gathering mist. On the damp, empty and unfamiliarly clean pavement in front of him a cat emerged from the upright railings of one of the smoothly tidy houses. It stalked, tail proudly erect, across the gleaming flat stones of the pavement, round the base of a lamp-post with a sinuous turn of its body, over the empty roadway and into the square garden.

Ghote stood and watched it, reflecting how differently it behaved from the slinking, mangy, vile cats of Bombay. The difference seemed to sum up for him the whole alteration in his surroundings in the past short forty-eight hours. He had come to a land where dignity had real meaning, to a land of law and order.

He straightened his back. He would do his small share

67

to preserve this law and order: he would if he possibly could bring the Peacock back to her appointed home.

Features set in an expression of high resolution, he marched off towards the Tagore House, turned the corner and strode hard along the narrow, less well-lit mews of the back-entrance. And in the gloom walked almost straight into a closely intertwined couple.

'Frigg off,' a muffled voice barked.

Ghote seized the latch of the Dattas' tall gate, tugged it hastily down and flung himself into the cluttered back garden.

Really, he thought, such behaviour. Kissing and hugging in a public place. Back at home he would have had the pair of them arrested in next to no time.

Standing breathing rather hard on the narrow brick path, he began to wonder whether the task that he had just pledged himself to was not going to be more complicated than it had started to seem.

He shrugged his shoulders, slipped the key as quietly as he could into the door in front of him and crept upstairs to continue his search of the possessions the Peacock had left behind her.

This time he was uninterrupted. But he made no discoveries.

Next evening Ghote left the conference meeting in a hurry, not displeased to have found a reason for avoiding Detective Superintendent Smart. He went by Underground straight to Royal Oak station, the nearest point according to his guide to the tower block of flats where both the two girls Policewoman Mackintosh had told him about lived. As he entered the ground-floor lobby of the towering, square-shouldered twenty-storey block, he felt the familiar tugging hunting instinct comfortably at work inside him. False trail it could still be, but he felt sure he was on to something. The Peacock must have had some reason for her sudden disappearance, and these two girls were almost bound to know something about it.

He glanced round. The bare lobby was, to his eyes, extraordinarily clean. No betel juice stains splattered the smooth grey walls, no huddled sleepers were taking advantage of the free shelter, there were no chips, cracks and dilapidation. Yet this was a block of Council flats, where the working-class lived. In such luxury as this the poor of mighty England dwelt.

His eye fell on the call-button for the two lifts. He pressed it. There was the soft hum of quietly working machinery, and a moment later one of the two aluminium doors in front of him slid open and the lift, a deep silver-walled square, was waiting.

He stepped in. The indicator board showed that both the flats he was looking for were up on the nineteenth floor. He pressed the button. The doors closed with a gentle thud. There was the slightest of shudderings and in less than a minute he had arrived.

The nineteenth floor landing was very much like the lobby below, clean and bare but thoroughly solid. There were four green-painted front doors for the four flats there. Ghote consulted the slip of paper Policewoman Mackintosh had given him and rang at the neat doorbell of the first of his two numbers.

He felt a little chill of expectation.

In a moment the door was opened. A smallish man of about fifty, very thin with neatly curling grey-white hair well brushed back above a fresh-looking face stood there. He wore an open-necked shirt, V-necked Fair Isle pull-over and slacks.

'Good evening,' Ghote said, 'I am looking for a Miss Patsy Morgan or a Miss Renee Timperley.'

'Patsy's my kid,' the man said. 'And Renee's in here with her, as per usual.'

Ghote drew breath to explain the reason for his visit. But with a sudden look of almost avaricious pleasure Mr Morgan shot out a sharp question.

'You're Indian, aren't you?' he said. 'Have you been here long?'

'Just two days,' Ghote answered cautiously.

'Ah,' said Mr Morgan, 'it's more than twenty years since I was in India. Do you know Barrackpore?'

'I am afraid not,' Ghote said. 'It is in Bengal, is it not? I am from Bombay. But, excuse me, I want – '

Mr Morgan took a pace forward and tapped him smartly on the chest with the fingers of his right hand.

'Finest troops in the Indian Army stationed at Barrack-pore,' he said. 'And I should know. I had the handling of 'em. Sergeant I was in those days. Sergeant Morgan, J. 1406231.'

He banged sharply to attention. And, had it not been that he was wearing slip-on, rubber-soled shoes, the effect would have been dramatic indeed.

Ghote smiled with as much sympathy as he could muster in face of his urgent need to talk to Mr Morgan's daughter.

'They must have been fine days,' he said. 'Only – '

'Fine days? They were the best days of my life. The best days of my life.'

Mr Morgan darted forward, swung round and fixed Ghote with a blazing-eyed look of distant enthusiasm.

'Imagine the scene,' he said. 'The drill square is here. To my left, cantonments for the native troops. To my right, sergeants' mess, cookhouse, etcetera. Straight ahead, officers' mess.'

'Oh, Dad, turn it in, do.'

The voice came from the open door of the flat. Both Mr Morgan and Ghote flicked round to face it as if on a single rotating platform.

Standing in the doorway were two girls of sixteen or seventeen dressed in neat, light grey school uniforms.

'Oh, Patsy,' Mr Morgan said, as soon as he had got his breath back. 'You got a visitor here, my girl. You and Renee. I was just recalling to him my time in India.'

'We heard,' said Patsy.

She was a short, fair-haired, plumpish girl with an air of about to go off at any second into a dazzle of bouncing like a pent-up rubber ball.

Behind her, her friend Renee, taller and darker and apparently quieter, was unable entirely to suppress a soft giggle.

Patsy looked at her father.

'I dare say they heard right down on the ground,' she added.

'Well, right down to the ground is where I'm going,' Mr Morgan replied. 'Down to the ground and out to the pub where I won't have no girls to bother me.'

He marched, proudly as once he had marched across the great drill square at Barrackpore, over and into the still waiting lift, and a moment later he was whisked out of sight.

'He's nuts, you know,' Patsy said to Ghote. 'Stark, staring, raving bonkers. I don't know why I put up with him.'

She stood in the doorway, giving him a pertly challenging look.

Ghote remained stern-faced. Then he grinned.

'At last I see what was the purpose of the British Raj,' he said. 'It is to keep girls like you amused.'

Patsy giggled. Unwillingly at first, but soon uncontrollably.

'No,' she said at last, 'but he can't get it off his mind, and he's very sweet really.'

The quieter Renee put in a word of her own.

'You came to see us about the Peacock, didn't you?' she said acutely.

'Yes, I did,' Ghote answered. 'You were both friends of hers, I think?'

'It was because of Reen really,' Patsy said eagerly. 'Because of the names. Renee and Ranee. Get it? I mean, that's how it all began. But as soon as we really got to

71

know her, then we knew we were going to be real friends for ever. Didn't we, Reen?'

The taller girl's eyes lit up.

'She was just marvellous,' she said. 'That's why we called her the Peacock. She was like something bright and dazzling sort of. Being with her was – was – '

She struggled for an image.

'It was like a party going on every minute of the day,' she said.

Plump, bouncy little Patsy's face went suddenly cloudy with tears.

'That's what makes it so awful,' she wailed.

'That she has gone?' Ghote said. 'I am here to try and find out exactly why she went, you know. I am a relative of hers, and a police officer back at home in India.'

The quiet Renee stepped forward.

'Can you find her?' she said. 'Do you think there's any hope? Or – '

She broke off.

'I am afraid I cannot make any guarantees by any means,' Ghote said soberly.

'I bet you can do more than that awful policewoman who came,' Patsy broke in, instantly alive again.

'I have met her,' Ghote said. 'She did not seem altogether happy about her interview with you.'

'She got so cross,' Patsy said.

She giggled.

'It was just a crack I made about police brutality,' she said. 'A friend of mine – Well, a friend of a sort of friend of mine got punched up in a police-station once. Or, anyhow, he thought he was going to get punched up. And he'd only been demonstrating about anti-apartheid or something.'

'And so you did not tell Policewoman Mackintosh what you know about the Peacock?' Ghote inquired.

He waited for the answer. Down in his stomach was the familiar feeling of tension.

It was the slightly more serious Renee who spoke for them both.

'It didn't seem much use telling someone like that,' she began. 'She'd have only gone and given us a lecture or something.'

She paused.

'And what was it you had to tell?' Ghote prompted.

'Well, really that she'd got the whole thing wrong.'

'Yes,' Patsy broke in, unable to keep out of things a moment longer. 'She began right off wanting a list of what she called "every single boy-friend" the Peacock had had. Cheek.'

'So we knew she wouldn't believe us if we said the Peacock had never had more than the one,' Renee explained.

'And then came the crack about brutality,' said Patsy.

A leaden feeling began growing up in Ghote's mind. Only one boy-friend: the signs were swinging round to point all together in the direction of Johnny Bull.

He fought against the tide a little.

'You know that the Peacock's aunt believes most strongly that she did not tell all her secrets to her friends,' he said.

'But of course she didn't,' Renee replied unexpectedly.

Ghote's hopes began to rise a little.

'No,' Renee went on, 'she didn't tell us things sometimes 'cos she liked giving surprises. She'd keep something secret for a day or two, and then bring it out with a bang like.'

'That was one of the things that made her fun,' Patsy added. 'Oh, I do wish she'd come back.'

'Still,' Renee said, picking up the thread earnestly, 'that sort of thing didn't mean she ever had real secrets from us. It goes to prove she didn't really, if you get me.'

Ghote did indeed get her.

'And it was Johnny Bull who was the one boy-friend?' he asked fatalistically.

'Oh, yes,' said Patsy, her eyes bright and her cheeks glowing with excitement. 'They were lovers. She seduced him in Calcutta, you know.'

Ghote was unable to keep a hint of disbelief from his features.

'Oh, go on, Patsy,' Renee said, with a touch of scornful impatience. 'You know it was the other way round really. She told us it was. Though she let him, of course.'

'She would,' Patsy said, all aglow. 'She was wonderful. So daring. So free.'

'That's what made it so sad.' Renee said. 'When he went off her.'

'He went off her?' Ghote asked, determined at least to keep the record absolutely straight.

'Yes,' said Patsy disgustedly. 'Some mean little bitch called Sandra got hold of him. I mean, she must have. Nobody could just get tired of her, not the Peacock.'

'I don't know, Pat,' Renee put in. 'I mean Johnny Bull's getting old. He must be nearly thirty. You get different then.'

'Yeah,' said Patsy. 'Can't keep up any more. I know.'

Ghote cautiously applied for further information.

'But the Peacock had not "gone off" Johnny Bull?' he asked.

'Oh, no,' said Patsy, as if the very suggestion smacked of treason.

'No, she hadn't, not a bit,' Renee confirmed. 'That was what was so awful for her. Poor kid.'

'It was terrible,' Patsy broke in, wild to have the telling of the romantic tale in her own hands. 'She couldn't stop loving that man, no more than a butterfly can stop singeing its wings in the candle-flame.'

'Moth, you mean,' said Renee with brisk scorn.

'Butterfly, moth, what's it matter? The thing is she'd have done anything to get him back. That's why she was so extra mad on new clothes and stuff. To win his love.'

Ghote considered for an instant.

74

'Has it occurred to you,' he said, 'that there may be a special reason for her disappearance?'

Patsy was quick.

'You mean to kind of scare Johnny?' she asked. 'Make him realise what he's lost?'

'That is what I was thinking.'

Patsy shook her head decisively.

'No,' she said. 'We talked about that, all three of us. But we reckoned it wouldn't do any good at all. A type like Johnny Bull's too selfish altogether to fall for that.'

'You wait till you meet him,' Renee said.

With a last sinking lurch, Ghote saw that this encounter was now inevitable.

'Well, I will wait until I have done that,' he said.

He regarded the two girls gravely. For all their happy chatter about sexual promiscuity, there was an untouched innocence about them still.

'There is something else,' he said.

They looked at him. Inquiry bright in their young faces.

'Sometimes girls of the Peacock's age take their own lives when they are in love,' he said.

Renee sombrely shook her dark head.

'No,' she said. 'If you think that, you just didn't know her very well.'

'I have never seen her,' Ghote admitted.

'Well then,' said Patsy heatedly, 'you just can't have any proper idea of her. She wouldn't go and kill herself. She was too alive for that. You can't see something bright and always shining turning and putting out its own light. Well, that was her, and she wouldn't do it.'

Renee added a characteristic note.

'She was too tough to,' she said. 'She could cope, that girl. That's what makes me –'

She came to an abrupt stop.

'Yes?' said Ghote quietly.

For some time she looked at him without speaking. Then she answered him, piecing together the words.

75

'The Peacock was tough,' she said, 'but I'm not. I mean, there are things I just won't let myself think about. I can't. And this is one of them.'

She turned impulsively towards Patsy.

'I haven't ever told you even, Pat.'

Patsy looked at her. The colour was noticeably draining even from her lively cheeks.

'You mean the chance that she may be dead?' she asked.

But Renee turned back to Ghote. Her eyes were shining with a deep current of emotion.

'If I let myself think about it,' she said, 'then I don't just wonder whether she's dead. I know it. Like as if it was in my bones, I know she is.'

Seven

Glumly Ghote marched next day along prosperous Sloane Street towards the tall Carlton Tower where Johnny Bull had his flat. The moment of encounter had come.

If the Peacock was dead, he asked himself for the hundredth time, who had killed her? It could have been some unknown, chance assailant. There was probably something in what Vidur Datta had once said about the dangers of London for an attractive, dazzling young girl. But, though London might not have vultures to scent out the dead, it was not very likely the body of the victim of such an attack would go undiscovered for three whole weeks.

So the only thing to do was to pick up the trail where it had apparently gone to ground: at Johnny Bull's. Because, for all his strong alibi, it was to him that the Peacock had decided to go. After her friends' testimony there could be no doubt that her 'lover' was Johnny.

He had come to this conclusion within a few minutes of leaving the girls the evening before, and had gone to bed that night in a fine old gloomy state in consequence. And with the new day he had contrived to find a series of excuses for putting off the inevitable encounter. The thought of the trouble it was almost bound to bring hung over him like a storm-cloud. Famous people when they feel themselves badgered are apt to hit out in all directions.

So first there had been his inescapable duty of making the very fullest notes at the conference. And, when he had been driven rapidly out of the imposing hall at Wood Street police-station by the possibility of meeting Detective Superintendent Smart, he had hit on yet one more delaying tactic. Stamping hard on his bad conscience, he had persuaded himself that he ought to get his present for Protima. After all, three days of his short stay had already gone by.

He went to a large department store, recommended by Mrs Datta with great vigour but without the backing of experience. It had been an unsettling business.

First, he had been unable to stop himself feeling a little overawed by the splendour of the place, with its marbled pillars, its cushiony carpeting and the careless magnificence and up-to-the-minute assurance of its pyramided displays. Then, when he had inquired several times for the china department and had at last found it, the assistant who had swept down on him had been a tall, firmly corseted goddess in a severe black dress with high-piled immaculately ordered golden hair who towered above him by a good twelve inches.

She had given him the coldest of smiles. He had said that he wanted a tea-set in Royal Worcester, 'a small tea-set.'

'War-cess-ter?' she had echoed, looking blankly puzzled.

It had taken them quite a long time to discover that he

should have been saying 'Wuster.' And then, with enormous rapidity and efficiency, he had been shown half a dozen different glittering sets. He had had difficulty making up his mind between them, but his assistant had had none.

'So the twenty-one pieces at nineteen, fifteen, three.'

Ghote had blinked.

Then he had realised that she was telling him the price. More than nineteen pounds. He did some fast arithmetic. One tea-set costing half a month's salary.

He had ventured to ask about 'something a little cheaper.' The high-piled, faultless golden hair had inclined majestically.

'We do not stock anything of that nature.'

And in face of all the calm of that pride, Ghote had simply turned tail.

So the antique shops of Sloane Street with their sombrely rich carpets on the window floors and their pieces of ancient, polished, superb furniture, solitary, spotlighted and stupendously priced, were more than a little depressing as he forced himself nearer and nearer to the meeting with Johnny Bull. Really, he had begun to dislike intensely certain features of the British way of life. Things were not by any means all as he had thought they would be. There were aspects of modern Britain that were not for him. Ever.

And, from all that he had heard, Johnny Bull was going to be another of those aspects.

Whirring smoothly up and up towards Johnny's flat in the black-walled, gold-decorated lift, he found he was inwardly chanting a repeated half-prayer, 'Let him be out, let him be out.'

He emerged from the lift. Directly in front of him was the door of Suite B. In the middle of the door was a discreet, stainless-steel bellpush. He tramped over and delicately put his finger on it. From somewhere inside came a subdued little hum.

And immediately the door was opened.

A girl stood there, her hand still resting on the latch. She must have been about eighteen, certainly not much more. She was small, with a round, pale, very soft-looking face framed in sleek colourless blonde hair. The features seemed hardly to make any impression. The nose was just a tiny blob; the mouth, bare of lipstick, was hardly more than an area of faint pinkness; the eyes floated, a watery blue, under the delicate smudge of her only make-up, a dab of bluish eye-shadow. She wore a frilly white blouse and a pale lilac-coloured skirt in some shiny material, very tight-fitting and hardly covering any of her softly plump legs at all.

Ghote decided that this must be the Sandra he had heard about.

'Yes?' she said, in a small, fluty, weary voice.

'I would like to see Mr Johnny Bull.'

She gave him a quick look, in which there was a tiny spark of irritation.

'So would a lot of people. What do you want?'

Ghote looked downwards for an instant.

'It is a personal matter,' he said.

'Listen. I'm the only personal matter Johnny's got. See?'

Ghote told himself firmly that even in Bombay he had been used to seeing as much of a woman's legs as this. He had seen the girls on Juhu Beach often enough wearing swimsuits that were in fact much more revealing than this skirt.

But somehow the garment's calculated effrontery did all the same seem plainly indecent.

'I am wanting to see Mr Bull about a relative of mine,' he said. 'A girl who has disappeared in mysterious –'

'Not her again.'

Sandra almost spat the words out for all her soft, fluty voice.

Ghote interrupted hastily.

79

'I know inquiries have already been made,' he said. 'But not much progress has been reported so far. I am actually an Indian police officer, here to attend a conference, an important conference. And I am making certain extra investigations. So if you would be so good.'

'Well, we've had all the investigation we want. Thank you very much.'

She began to close the door.

With only the slightest reluctance, Ghote put his foot against the jamb.

'Please listen,' he said. 'I am not here to make trouble. It is just that the people the girl lived with have got it into their heads that Mr Bull is in some way to blame.'

'In some way to blame? Listen, mate, they told Johnny to his face that he's keeping her locked up here, in his harem or something.'

It came as a surprise to Ghote that the Dattas had been in direct contact with Johnny Bull. No doubt the approach had not been a success.

'Yes, yes,' he said quickly. 'Most regrettable. Quite wrong. Please do not think I believe anything like that myself.'

Podgy little Sandra stopped trying to push the door shut.

'What do you believe then?' she asked.

'I do not believe anything,' Ghote pleaded. 'I am just trying to find out the truth.'

But Sandra's pallid blue eyes remained mulishly obstinate.

Over her shoulder Ghote looked at the interior of Johnny's flat. There was a wide corridor painted a plain white and hung with the trophies of the great man's career – record sleeves, posters and, in a place of honour, a golden disc.

'Well, you can go and find the truth somewhere else,' Sandra said. 'We don't know a thing about your precious Peacock here. I wouldn't have her within a mile of the place, not after I arrived.'

She gave her pert little bosom under the frilly white blouse an aggressive tilt upwards and looked challengingly at Ghote.

He realised that he would have to sink his pride a certain amount.

'But it is not only for my sake,' he said. 'It is for Johnny's also.'

'Johnny's?'

'Listen, no one could be a bigger fan for Johnny Bull than I am, and all this is going to be bad for him. Bad publicity.'

A look of calculation arrived on the soft, pudgy face in front of him.

'You really a fan?'

'Am I really a fan?'

Ghote succeeded in infusing his voice with rich enthusiasm. He looked straight ahead past the girl's shoulder.

'Look,' he said, 'I think Johnny's rendering of "Love, love, love" is the greatest.'

The record-sleeve was not two yards away from him. It was easy. And Indian magazines' delighted imitations of the jargon of British and American fans were almost inescapable in Bombay.

'Yeah,' Sandra agreed. 'That disc was all right.'

'And "It's Love, Only Love." That was another magnificent disc, even though it was some time ago.'

Underneath each record-sleeve on the white wall was a black label with a date in gold figures.

Ghote rushed on.

'And going back a bit further, when there were all those great successes. Things like "Going to My Lover Today." That was really a hit.'

'Got him a gold disc, that did,' Sandra said offhandedly.

And Ghote knew that he had won. He allowed himself the pleasure of reflecting tartly on all the harping on sentimental love that had brought Johnny his success. Really, at times the West was just disgusting.

Sandra swung the door wide open in front of him.

'You'd better come in,' she said. 'If all this is going to bring my boy bad publicity, we'll have to see what can be done.'

'We certainly will,' Ghote chimed in enthusiastically. 'Nothing must be allowed to interfere with a great career.'

'You're telling me,' said Sandra.

She swung round and walked away along the corridor.

'I'll just make sure he's got his clothes on, my Johnny,' she said.

In the tight mini-skirt her hips swayed like a pair of nicely inflated balloons. She went through a door at the far end.

Ghote stood straining to hear. There was the sound of voices, Sandra's hardly audible at all and a deep male one, saying little. He caught an occasional half-phrase. 'Oh, all right,' 'Quick about it.' Then the door at the end of the wide, thickly carpeted corridor opened. Sandra swung her head round it.

'He says to come in,' she called.

Advancing towards her over the springy white carpeting, Ghote tried to hide the anxiety he felt under a look of radiant anticipation.

Sandra hauled the door open to its widest.

The room that Ghote entered was long with a stretch of windows all down one side, looking out on to the tops of trees, bare twisted branches with here and there a greeny-yellow leaf still clinging. Under this window was a big square sofa covered in rough-textured chocolate-brown material. A long, low coffee table stood in front of it with a scattering of sheets of manuscript music on it, weighted down by a big green glass ash-tray.

Then at the far end of the room his eye was caught by an object that struck him with an odd pang of familiarity. Looking sad, battered and totally incongruous on the spotless deep-pile white wall-to-wall carpet, was, of all things, an ancient harmonium. It was just the sort of instrument common in India, a curious take-over from the missionaries, seized on as a useful and portable way of making music.

As he looked up from it with a frown of slight puzzlement, he saw Johnny.

The well-loved singer was leaning idly back in a big, low-slung arm-chair, brother to the huge sofa. He was, it was at once obvious, a creature of bold handsomeness. Tall, well over six foot as he lay sprawled in the big chair, he wore a long coat in a very dark grey material, cut very closely fitting. It showed up, for all the careless ease of his attitude, a tautly slim waist and wide set powerful shoulders. His legs, which were long and well-shaped, were encased in very tightly fitting trousers of the same material as the coat. Beneath, his feet were bare except for a pair of heel-less black leather slippers.

His face was long and darkish complexioned with good, bold features and dark brown, deeply set, eyes. A mane of dark hair curled a little over his jutting forehead and swept thickly backwards down to the very collar of his odd-looking coat.

He did not move when Ghote turned to him.

'Good evening,' Ghote said carefully. 'It is very good of you to see me.'

'I need to see you, feller,' Johnny Bull said.

He had a deep, rather resonant voice. Ghote decided not to be put out by the hint of a sneer in it.

'Yes, Mr Bull,' he said quietly, 'I think you do need my help. I tell you frankly – '

'Mr Bull?' said Sandra from the doorway. 'Call him Johnny. You got to call that boy Johnny.'

'I tell you frankly,' Ghote ploughed on, 'that I am most worried about what effect these rumours will have on a fine career.'

Johnny Bull suddenly swung upright in his big square chair.

'Damn and blast it,' he said, his voice less deep now,

'damn and blast it, why does this have to happen to me now? Now of all times?'

His fine dark eyes clouded with pain, like a hurt child's. He darted a look up at Ghote.

'Oh, bloody sit down, man, for heaven's sake,' he snapped.

Ghote sat on the edge of the deep, chocolate-brown sofa.

'This is a bad time for you?' he asked.

And something which had been tapping at his senses ever since he had entered the luxurious though somehow bare room succeeded abruptly in registering itself. There was a faint but definite odour everywhere, an odd, half-sweet, half-acrid smell which he felt he recognised but which he could not at that moment place.

He pushed the nagging query it raised firmly to the back of his mind and listened attentively to Johnny.

'Of course it's a bad time for me. It's the image. Don't you know?'

'Your image is having a bad time?' Ghote asked, stepping as delicately as he could.

'I thought you were meant to be a fan?'

Johnny made no attempt to conceal the note of hostile suspicion.

'But I am a fan,' Ghote said with a touch of desperation. 'I am a most keen admirer, most damnably keen.'

Johnny looked him up and down along the length of his beautifully straight nose.

'If you say so,' he answered. 'But it takes all sorts.'

'Oh, but, yes,' Ghote said earnestly. 'I assure you, you have many followers in India among people of my generation.'

'India,' said Johnny, 'that's it. India's the new image I was talking about.'

He darted Ghote a sudden newly suspicious glance.

'But you ought to know that, if you're a fan,' he said. 'It's been in all the papers.'

'Ah, that accounts for it,' Ghote said quickly. 'I have had little time to read the papers recently. I was sent over here at very short notice, to attend an important conference.'

'Yeah?'

Johnny could not have conveyed less interest. He shifted himself a little more upright.

'I'll tell you how it is with me,' he said.

A shine of excitement sprang up in his deep-set eyes.

'When the career began,' he said, 'it couldn't have gone better than it did. That golden disc came at just the right time. After it I couldn't cut records fast enough. They wanted me everywhere, the London Palladium, Reno night-clubs, everything. Those were the days, the great days.'

He came to a halt. His eyes had taken on a deep, dreamy look. After a little Ghote felt obliged to give him a slight nudge.

'But now there is the problem of your image?' he said.

Johnny's sensual mouth curled disgustedly.

'They began to drift away, the fans,' he said. 'They thought I was getting too old. I'm twenty-five, over twenty-five. I don't disguise it. But I had to do something. So that's when I got that thing.'

With the toe of one dangling black leather slipper he indicated the old harmonium against the far wall.

'It is a harmonium?' Ghote asked with double caution.

'Yeah, it's a harmonium all right. You ought to know, I picked it up in your neck of the woods. It's a genuine old Indian harmonium.'

'Most interesting.'

'But that's my new sound, feller. The Indian sound. And then there's the Indian look. That's why I got me this new gear.'

With a long-fingered, well-manicured hand he patted his dark grey, close-fitting, high-buttoned coat. Ghote saw that it was indeed a version of the familiar *atchkan*, much popularised by such figures as Pandit Nehru.

'It's all going to do it,' Johnny said. 'Bring the old career right up to those heights again. The Indian look, the Indian sound and a touch of that old Kama Sutra stuff in the publicity. Just the hint, you know. Just the tip that bed with Johnny boy is something you don't come across every day of the week.'

Sandra, standing attentively by the door, giggled softly. She came across and sat on the broad arm of Johnny's chair and leant nuzzlingly towards him.

'Yes. Publicity,' said Ghote sharply.

Johnny pushed Sandra morosely aside and sat up.

'It's hell this publicity business,' he said sorrowfully. 'You'd think, wouldn't you, that nothing would be better than having the tale go round that I kept a slave-girl or two. But I tell you, it'd be death. Death.'

'Death?' said Ghote.

'Death to the image, feller. Policemen hanging round, inquiries, all that. It's nasty. The fans don't like it. The record companies don't like it. There's nothing worse.'

'So we must find out what has happened to the Peacock,' said Ghote decisively.

'The Peacock,' Johnny said thoughtfully. 'It wasn't a bad name for the kid, you know. She was a dresser all right. She paraded her charms for all to see. I can make a guess at what happened to her.'

'The bitch,' said Sandra.

Johnny smiled up at her lazily.

'All women are bitches,' he said.

'One moment, please,' Ghote said sharply. 'We are getting away from the problem. What is important for you is to make it completely plain that you could not have had anything to do with the Peacock's disappearance. Can you prove that?'

'But I was telling you, feller – ' Johnny began.

'Where were you on the night of October the twenty-first last?' Ghote shot out at him.

Johnny looked at him, his eyes widening.

'The night of October the twenty-first,' he said. 'You sound like a detective or something.'

'I am a detective,' Ghote said.

Johnny blinked.

'Oh, yeah,' he said, 'Sandra told me. Indian detective. Somehow I never thought they had 'em.'

'We do,' Ghote replied, not allowing himself to be riled. 'And when someone has disappeared, they ask questions. Questions like: what were you doing on the night of October the twenty-first last?'

Lazing back in the big, square, chocolate-coloured chair, Johnny looked at him with a hint of a grin.

'Feller,' he said. 'I haven't the least idea when the night of the twenty-first was, nor the twenty-second, nor the twenty-third.'

'The twenty-first was the day the Peacock disappeared,' Ghote said. 'Trafalgar Day.'

'Trafalgar Day, was it? Then I'll tell you what I must have been doing: climbing Nelson's Column to celebrate.'

'This is no time for joking,' Ghote said. 'Please remember, the answers you give might put a rope round your neck.'

But Johnny, lying back in the big chair with one black leather slipper flipping and flapping at the end of an extended foot, was not impressed.

'Not a rope, feller,' he said. 'This is an enlightened, civilised country. We don't hang people no more.'

Ghote fought down his annoyance. He ploughed on.

'Very well. Perhaps you would be good enough to tell me exactly what were your feelings towards my cousin – towards the Peacock in the days preceding her disappearance?'

'Just the same as they had been for the past couple of months. If you must know.'

And the black leather slipper flipped insolently up and down.

'And what had they been in that period, if you please?'

Johnny looked at him straight down the length of his straight, straight nose.

'I was stinking fed up with the cow,' he said.

Ghote reflected with modest pleasure that, engrossed in his task, he was able to ignore completely the calculated insult to someone asking about a relative in distress.

'You were fed up with her?' he replied sedately. 'Why was this?'

Sandra, snuggling closer than ever into Johnny's side, answered for him.

'Why was this?' she mimicked. 'This was because I came along.'

'You get to need a change once in a while,' Johnny explained carelessly.

'Not any more you don't,' Sandra said.

Johnny slowly rose to an upright position in the big chair. He twisted round a little and looked the softly plump little Sandra in the face.

'Get,' he said.

She promptly attempted to wind herself round his chest, making a little cooing, murmuring noise. He grasped her two elbows with his large, well-formed hands, gripped hard and peeled her off like a length of sticky plant-tendril.

'Get out,' he said, with theatrically quiet menace.

Sandra blinked her pallid eyes.

'Yes, Johnny boy,' she said.

Johnny, back almost flat in the chocolate-coloured chair, watched her in silence as she walked the length of the room and went out, carefully closing the door behind her.

'You have to keep them in their place,' he said. 'If they get out of hand they cause no end of trouble.'

'And the Peacock caused no end of trouble?' Ghote asked.

Johnny smiled. The black slipper began to flip to and fro again in a maddeningly slow irregular rhythm.

'The Peacock caused trouble,' he said. 'And that was the simple reason I wouldn't see her any more.'

'But she forced her way in?'

Johnny shook his head from side to side.

'No, feller. She did not.'

Undismayed, Ghote tried a small experiment.

'She did not try to see you,' he said, 'even though she was with child?'

For a little Johnny did not reply. But the black slipper flipped and flopped.

Then he grinned.

'You wouldn't be trying it on, would you?' he said. 'I don't remember hearing anything about anything like that when I had that angry old uncle character on the phone. And I'd have thought he'd do a big line over his little girlie being "with child".'

A vision of Vidur Datta sombrely indignant over such an outrage came into Ghote's head. Johnny certainly was armed with plenty of shrewdness.

But for form's sake he held to his line a little longer.

'You are not denying that the Peacock could have been with child by you?'

Johnny shrugged.

'Do I sound like I'm denying?' he said. 'But if you ask me that girl was a pretty slick chick. She wouldn't have gone getting herself into that sort of trouble. She knew her way around.'

'But if all the same she had got herself into that sort of trouble,' Ghote persisted. 'She could have made things most unpleasant for you?'

Johnny shook his head.

'Now that's the sort of publicity that does no harm at all,' he said. 'Nice little affiliation order or two, makes the girls know you really mean business. Same as when they slap a fine on you for what they call "possession of dangerous drugs." Then everybody knows you're a real swinger.'

And with the words 'dangerous drugs' Ghote realised

in the space of less than a second what exactly the curious odour he had noticed on first coming in was. It was the smell of opium. The highly characteristic, sweet yet acrid smell of opium. If he had not been able to place it instantly, it was only because he had never expected to encounter it anywhere in England. In Bombay he had smelt the unmistakable tang often enough in the course of his duties, even before he had joined Superintendent Ketkar's department. In places like the crowded district behind the commercial dignity of the Fort area, as you pushed your way along the noisy, narrow lanes, every now and again you came across it, even seeping out into the open. And there would be a fifth-rate eating-house with a narrow flight of stairs at the back and a signboard in front of it in English and Chinese. You might raid it with a team of tough constables and you would find half a dozen Chinese-born seamen stretched out in the faraway languor that comes after smoking what they called *chandu* and what is known in Hindi as *afim*, opium.

But to come across that odour here in England, this was a different matter.

He leapt to his feet and pointed accusingly at the reclining figure of Johnny Bull.

'Opium,' he said. 'You make use of opium.'

And flip, flop went the dangling black slipper.

'You want a couple of smokes?' Johnny said.

Ghote checked himself. He was letting his sense of outrage at what was being done in this land he admired run away with him. It would not get him anywhere with his inquiry to denounce Johnny Bull as a vile degenerate.

'No,' he said, sitting quietly down again, 'I am merely a little surprised that this is the drug you choose.'

Johnny smiled comfortably.

'It's going to be the one they all choose soon,' he said. 'Yeah, give it a year or two and coke and L.S.D. and all that lot will be for squares. The pipe's going to be the thing. It's got class, and it's real dreamy to use.'

'You have been using it long?'

'Since my trip to India, feller. Came across it in Bombay. You ever in Bombay?'

'I work there.'

'And you don't smoke? You're missing something, feller.'

Ghote ignored the lazy jibe.

'The smoking of opium is illegal in this country,' he said.

'So are lots of other nice things that don't do any harm.'

Johnny grinned impudently. Ghote decided not to give him a lecture about the long-term effects of opium-smoking.

'Where do you obtain your supplies from?' he asked casually. 'Did you bring them in bulk from Bombay?'

His professional interest was aroused. This might be a useful way of improving his stock at the conference.

'Now don't be stupid, feller,' Johnny said. 'You think I'd risk bringing in that stuff. You get prison for that. No, I buy myself a little bit whenever I need it.'

He gave Ghote a decidedly sharp look.

'But I thought you were meant to be finding out what happened to that Peacock girl of yours?'

'And what do you think happened to her yourself?' Ghote shot quickly back.

But Johnny simply smiled again.

'I haven't the slightest idea what's happened to her,' he said. 'And what's more I don't care. India will do fine to give a bit of new life to the old image, but don't let me have any more to do with Indians. They're so crawly I could stamp on them.'

'But you are British,' Ghote said, 'a fine British singer making lots of money and keeping British records on all the hit parades?'

The contented look stayed on Johnny's face.

'You've said it, feller,' he answered.

'Then let me tell you something,' Ghote snapped. 'I

have seen your like by the dozen in India. You are nothing but a typical playboy Indian film-star. I have had dealings with them in plenty, and most of them are nothing but spoilt brats.'

And the last shot got home. Johnny's dark eyes narrowed in sudden fury. He opened his mouth to reply and found nothing to say.

Ghote jumped up and headed for the door.

But before he reached it Johnny Bull found his tongue.

'All right,' he said. 'All right, Mister Bloody High-and-mighty. But let me tell you something about your precious relative, something that'll come as news to you.'

Ghote turned.

Johnny was sitting on the very edge of the big chocolate-brown chair now. He was bolt upright and shaking with rage.

'Your precious Peacock,' he said, 'was nothing but a low-down little drugger. I may smoke because I need it for my work, but she just drugged to make herself lower than she was. She went down to that place off the Portobello Road, the Robin's Nest, and did anything, anything in the world, to lay her hands on whatever she could get.'

Eight

Hurrying away from the Carlton Tower along the now glowingly lit and even more implacably opulent Sloane Street, Ghote had been tempted to seek out the place called the Robin's Nest, whatever it was, at once. He would have liked to find out at the earliest possible moment just where what he had heard from Johnny Bull was going to lead him.

But within a few minutes he had come to the conclusion

92

that it would be better to approach the whole matter with some caution. For one thing, he had only the scantiest information to go on. It would have been useless to have asked Johnny for further details.

What was clear was that his accusation was basically true: he had got too much satisfaction out of making it for it to have been something which was going to get disproved. Ghote wondered what Mr and Mrs Datta were going to say when they heard.

He found them both comfortably installed in their wilfully Indian sitting-room, Mrs Datta busy with some sewing and Cousin Vidur standing in front of the popping little gas fire, with the ranks of laxative bottles and packets on the mantelpiece ranged comfortingly behind him.

As soon as Ghote came in, Vidur began to deliver himself of a few observations which he seemed to have been storing up for just such an occasion.

'Well, Cousin Ganesh,' he said, 'and what do you think of these English, now that you have seen them in their own country for a little? A pretty rotten lot, isn't it? Wearing the mini-skirt, eating beef.'

He looked down severely in the direction of his own solid little belly, not one ounce of which could be attributed to nourishment derived from anything even half as sacred as the cow.

'I tell you,' he continued, 'I cannot wait for the day when I can sell this place, lock, stock and barrel, and go back to the ancient decencies of our native land.'

A visionary gleam came into his two little eyes.

'And that may not be too long now,' he said. 'We thought we were in for a bad setback when they abolished the tax allowance for expense-account entertaining. But in the end it came to nothing. In a few months the bar returns were one hundred per cent back to normal.'

Ghote, in spite of the fact that his views on British life seemed now to have got much closer to Cousin Vidur's, decided that he was not prepared to voice a note of sympathy. He need not have pondered the matter.

'Yes,' Vidur hammered on with scarcely a pause, 'it is a degenerate, religionless land we have to earn our poor living in. Drinking alcoholic liquors, kissing in the public streets, driving here, there and everywhere in fast cars. There is no end to it, no end at all. And then, the night-clubs. Open to all hours, displays of women in all their nakedness, taking the business from places that have the right to it. Disgusting, thoroughly disgusting.'

'I know what you mean,' Ghote cut in quickly.

He had seen a chance of sounding out the Dattas on what he had learnt about the Peacock and was determined to take it.

'It is not only alcohol,' he went on quickly. 'There is drug-taking too. I hear that – '

'Yes, certainly,' Vidur broke in forcefully. 'It is a nation of drug-addicts also. Cocaine, heroin, stuff from America that has the most undesirable effects. The whole thing is rife everywhere.'

'Are drugs easy to obtain here then?' Ghote snapped in.

'Oh, yes, yes. They are sold in the streets. It is common knowledge.'

'In any particular area?' Ghote asked. 'I heard mention of the Portobello Road. Is that what they call it? Where-abouts is that?'

Mrs Datta answered. She could no longer bear not to have a part in such a vigorously denunciatory conver-sation.

'The Portobello Road is not far from here,' she said. 'There is a market for antiques and a vegetable market. Once I used to buy vegetables there, but when I started to take my Peacock with me I found I had all the time been cheated.'

'The Peacock knew the area then?' Ghote asked quickly.

94

Mrs Datta drew herself up proudly on the low divan where she was sitting.

'All London she knew,' she said. 'Piccadilly Circus, Trafalgar Square, Carnaby Street. Everywhere.'

But something in the way Ghote had put his question had alerted Vidur Datta.

'Why do you ask if the girl knew that area?' he said, with a quick glance from his shrewd eyes embedded in their dense flesh.

Ghote drew a deep breath.

'Because of something I learnt when I visited Johnny Bull this evening,' he said.

'You have visited Johnny Bull?' Mrs Datta said, immediately agog.

'What was this you learnt?' her husband asked, more pertinently.

Ghote looked at him squarely.

'I learnt that the Peacock was in the habit of obtaining drugs from a place off the Portobello Road called the Robin's Nest,' he said. 'Do you know where that is?'

'No,' said Vidur Datta. 'Certainly not.'

'But it is a café,' Mrs Datta said sharply. 'You must know it. You have often been to the Portobello Road, and it is easy to see as you walk along.'

And, to Ghote's fury, a classically interminable family argument promptly broke out. The question of the Peacock being a drug-buyer was completely ignored. Instead the likelihood of Vidur Datta having noticed a café a few yards off the Portobello Road reigned supreme. With the greatest vehemence, he maintained that he could have no notion of where the place could be and that in any case he had hardly ever even been to the Portobello Road. With unending persistence, his wife claimed that he could not have failed to have seen the café, if he had walked only once along the length of the narrow market-street, and that in point of fact he had been there many times. She got down to dates and occasions.

'I tell you it is not so,' Cousin Vidur declared, fiercely astride on his two plump little legs. 'Once or twice I may have been. But if I was it was for business only. I did not want to go looking into cheap eating-houses and brothels.'

'The Robin's Nest is not brothel,' Mrs Datta retorted, giving her husband a furious glare through her steel-rimmed spectacles. 'It is a café, and very well you know it.'

'Café, brothel. Brothel, café. They are all the same these places,' Vidur pronounced.

He glared at his wife.

'But I have no time to be talking all this,' he added sharply. 'Someone has to perform religious duties in this house.'

And, stamp, stamp, stamp, he crossed over the bare floor and marched out.

Mrs Datta turned to Ghote.

'I tell you,' she said with vehemence, 'that café is ten yards only from the Portobello Road.'

Ghote however was not going to get embroiled in that argument.

'And do you think it is likely the Peacock got drugs there?' he asked brutally.

The question had the deflating effect he had hoped for.

Mrs Datta sat on the edge of the low couch and blinked at him behind her sharply askew spectacles.

'I do not know,' she said quietly at last.

'You saw no signs?'

Again Mrs Datta blinked.

'It is possible,' she said. 'I do not know what are the signs of drugs. But in the last few weeks she was sometimes very gay and excited, though she is the sort of girl who is often very excited.'

She sat silent and thoughtful.

Ghote did not think there would be much more she could tell him. He watched her, wondering whether there was anything he ought to do to help her. She had held the Peacock so highly that even the suspicion that the girl's high spirits had led her into the world of the drug-takers must be a sharp blow.

At last she looked up.

'And Johnny Bull?' she asked. 'What else did he say?'

'He confirmed what the policewoman and detective-sergeant who went to see him had found out,' Ghote answered, as sympathetically as he could.

'And you asked no more than they did?' Mrs Datta said.

There was an edge to the remark. But Ghote decided to ignore it.

'I do not know exactly every question they asked,' he said. 'But I myself saw enough to be certain that Johnny Bull and this girl he has would have been together for the whole of the time the Peacock disappeared. She is a most possessive girl. Most.'

'But why did you not ask more?' Mrs Datta said.

She cocked her head sharply to one side. Her spectacles glinted fiercely.

Ghote found that he was beginning to be a little irked. Who was this restaurant-keeper's wife to go querying the methods of an inspector of the C.I.D.?

'But please understand,' he said. 'Questions to Johnny Bull are no longer necessary. The new factor in the case puts a completely different complexion on the whole matter.'

Mrs Datta shook her head in bland negative.

'What you have to do,' she said, 'is to get my Peacock back from that Johnny Bull.'

And suddenly Ghote had the sensation of being asked to fight his way through a dense black, impenetrable mass pressing in on him from every side. He made one gigantic effort.

'Listen,' he almost screamed out, 'listen, if anything has happened to the Peacock, it is because she was involved with a lot of drug addicts. At this café called the Robin's Nest. And just as soon as I can I am going to go round there and find out exactly what she did, who she saw and what she said. And then perhaps we will begin to get at the truth.'

But it was not until well into the evening of the next day that Ghote was able to set out for the Robin's Nest. On this of all occasions the organisers of the Drugs Conference had elected to fit in one more paper than usual, and in consequence the meeting was not over until after six o'clock. Ghote had fumed and fretted, but there was nothing he could do about it. Superintendent Ketkar had the programme of papers and he would expect notes as comprehensive on one as on any other. And there was already the missing part of the first paper of all to be accounted for somehow.

So it was just seven o'clock when eventually Ghote arrived at the top end of the twisting market-street. Thrusting his guide book into an outside pocket of his great hairy coat, he looked all round about him. The street looked narrow, deserted and a little ominous in front of him, its shabby-looking houses dwarfed by the distant skyline pricked out by scattered patches of lights. Ghote thought he recognised one of these, a tall rectangle, as the tower block of Council flats where he had met Patsy and Renee, those giggly but attractive representatives of the New Britain, and had first begun seriously to consider the possibility that the Peacock was dead.

He turned back to the narrow street in front of him. Perhaps before long he would learn something to lead him to whoever it was who had killed her. He began walking slowly forward.

At this hour only a litter of discarded vegetables, fruit and wrapping-paper showed where the market-stalls had been earlier in the day. But the windows of some of the small shops had lights in them and their higgledy-piggledy miscellany of bric-à-brac was attracting an occasional passer-by to stop and stare in at them in a melancholy way for a moment or two. Ghote looked at one of them himself.

What could anybody possibly want with an old, old horn-gramophone obviously jammed into silence years ago? He twisted his head round till he could read the price on the tiny little white ticket attached to the handle. It ran into pounds. He left the window abruptly and walked hurriedly off.

He kept a good look-out to either side for the Robin's Nest, though, if what Mrs Datta had said was true, it should not be hard to spot. He looked at one or two small, unpretentious cafés, but they were all on the street itself.

And then, just before he got to a big old public-house, the Warwick Castle, he saw it.

Mrs Datta appeared to have had justice on her side in the argument with her husband: the Robin's Nest was very obvious. It was only a few yards up a side-turning, a small place, but brightly enough lit. With its name painted up above it in crudely bright red letters it would be hard to miss.

Ghote turned into the side-street and made a casual-seeming inspection from across the narrow roadway. Compared with the restaurants and tea-shops he had seen round Marble Arch and in the City, the Robin's Nest was unprepossessing. It consisted of a single room of moderate size with a dozen small tables in it jutting out from the walls and set rather too closely together for comfort. Through the steamy glass of its single shop-window, Ghote could see only one customer and a vague figure flitting about behind a counter at the far end.

This would be the ideal time to go in and ask questions.

He crossed the road. On the glass door of the café was an inexpertly painted robin chiefly notable for the extreme brightness of its red breast. He put his hand on the glass just above it and pushed. The door opened with a clucking sort of ping from its bell.

The one customer, a white-faced, depressed-looking youth in a grubby fawn mackintosh sitting near the door, just glanced up and then buried himself again in his evening paper. In front of him there was a half-full cup of tea. The cup was of thick white china and looked very small.

Making his way up to the counter at the far end, Ghote was struck by the painstaking efforts that had been made everywhere to brighten up the tattered framework of the place.

The tops of the tables had been covered in patterned plastic, mostly red with a design of yellow circles. But evidently this material had run out, because one of the two tables nearest the counter was blue with a pattern of red stars. The wooden chairs had been painted a gay shade of red too, though even at a casual glance it was clear the painter was no professional. Along the row of shelves behind the counter brightly patterned paper – yellow bells on a green background – had been carefully pinned, and its edges had been neatly trimmed with a pair of serrated scissors. On the shelves, the bottles of soft drinks were ranged in clumps of contrasting shades.

Pinned to the walls, which had recently been papered in blue and white stripes, already splodged here and there with grease stains, were three hand-written notices, each done in bold but uneven letters in green ink and each carrying a version of the inexpertly drawn robin on the door. One said 'No Dogs Allowed – Please,' the next 'Gentlemen are Kindly requested NOT to kick the juke box' and the third 'Why not try a Lolly Cola. New. Refreshing. DIFFerent.'

The juke box, which was jammed up against one end of the counter, looked as if it had nevertheless received plenty of kicks in the course of a long life of gradual decline. But even here something had been done to restore some of the original spruceness. A fresh line of bold red paint had been applied all round the top edge, the criss-cross battlefield of the metal parts had been devotedly polished and on the top of the whole there had been placed a bright blue bird-cage. In this there sat, rather huddled and morose, a real-live robin.

The man behind the counter had somewhat the same air as the juke box – of having had a hard time of it but of being determined to stay spry.

He was aged about fifty and was a good deal below medium height and decidedly tubby. He had a round, ruddy face, with a little hook of a nose jutting out in the middle of it and sparse auburn hair brushed to the best advantage across a balding, red, round skull. He wore a blue-and-white striped apron round his little tummy with, above it, a plum-coloured waistcoat with brass buttons.

As Ghote came up, he put down a cup he had been drying.

'And for you, sir?' he said chirpily.

'Good evening,' Ghote said, with deliberately careful slowness, 'do you serve coffee here?'

'Straight from the big tin, sir. Tenpence a cup.'

'Thank you. Thank you. That will be excellent.'

He watched while Robin – for there was such an air of proprietorship about him that he could be none other than the owner of Robin's Nest – dipped under the counter, produced the big tin of coffee powder, scooped out one precise measureful, tipped it neatly into a cup and held it under the little brass tap of the dented chromium hot-water urn on the counter.

After a little Ghote proffered another remark in the character he had assumed.

'I have been strolling along your Portobello Road,' he said, 'but I was regretful to find all the market stalls had gone.'

'Ah, yes,' said Robin brightly, 'pack up any time round half past five, they do. But if it's antiques and curiosities you're after, and many foreign gentlemen are, then you want to come on a Saturday. Saturday morning, Saturday afternoon, all the same thing.'

Ghote noted with pleasure that at least his impersonation had been accepted.

'On Saturday, I will remember,' he said. 'I have heard a great deal about the Portobello Road, and I am curious to see it myself in full swing.'

'And well worth seeing too, if you'll take my advice,' Robin replied, cocking his head knowingly to one side. 'You wait till Saturday. Fine old crowd you'll find here then, poking and prying among all the barrows and in the shops. And you can pick up anything here. Anything. Gentleman found a genuine Rembrandt the other day. Brought it in here, he did. Proud as Punch. Didn't think all that much to it myself. Just a grey old thing, it was. Like a bit of colour, I do.'

He looked round with shining pleasure at the bit of colour he had superimposed on the shoddy framework of his Nest.

Ghote saw his chance of moving the conversation one step nearer his goal.

'You certainly seem to have made this place most colourful, most agreeable.'

Robin blushed with delight.

'Not too bad,' he said. 'Haven't been here all that long, mind. But it certainly needed a lick or two of paint when I came along.'

Ghote put down his coffee and carried out a long inspection. The depressed-looking youth by the door had sidled out and the place was empty. But, except for the one empty cup and abandoned chewed-looking newspaper, everything was as spick and span as wiping and polishing could make it.

''Course,' Robin went on, 'there's a lot wants doing to it yet, when I find the time. And the money. Needs a bit of capital outlay, this place does, really. And that's not so easy to come by.'

'Quite so, quite so,' said Ghote heartily. 'But all the same, it has a very nice appearance even now. I would not be at all surprised if it does not attract a good many of my countrymen. We are very particular about cleanliness in India, you know.'

'Indians?' Robin answered. 'Yes, I get one or two Indians come in from time to time. Always sure of a good welcome here, they are. Every creed and colour welcome at Robin's Nest, I say.'

He preened himself.

'Yes, yes,' said Ghote eagerly. 'I am sure it would be most pleasing to them to come here.'

He leant a little farther across the counter.

'And there is something you might be able to tell me about that,' he said.

'Anything to oblige,' said Robin. 'That's my motto: anything to oblige.'

'I have a relative over here,' Ghote said. 'A girl, about seventeen. I understand she was fond of coming to this particular area, and unfortunately she was disappeared from home. I wonder if you ever saw her in here?'

On the far side of the shiningly polished counter, Robin's face abruptly lost every trace of geniality.

He turned sharply away and picked up the cup he had finished drying as Ghote had come up. He took a tea-towel and began vigorously rubbing at it with his back turned.

'Can't say I recollect anyone of that nature,' he said. 'Definitely not.'

Ghote's stomach tautened a little with the scent of a quarry.

He pushed aside his cup of coffee, which he had been carefully spinning out, and went quickly along the short length of the counter until he had Robin cornered next to the dented chromium urn.

'Now,' he said, 'you will answer some questions, and you will answer quickly.'

103

Robin shot him a half-defiant glance over his shoulder.

'I've got work to do,' he said. 'I can't be answering questions all night for a lot of bloody foreigners.'

'What was that girl's name?' Ghote snapped back.

This time Robin did not turn at all.

'You should know her name,' he muttered. 'Why ask me?'

'Because you know and you are going to tell me,' Ghote replied in a tone of patience-nearly-at-the-end-of-its-tether which he copied from his old teacher Mr Merry-wether and had used to effect on other occasions.

'But I don't know,' Robin said petulantly.

'You do. Now, what is it?'

Robin's reply was scarcely audible. But Ghote did not need to hear every syllable.

'They called her the Peacock or something, if you must know.'

'Exactly,' Ghote barked. 'They called her the Peacock. Now, why did she keep coming in here?'

Robin swung round.

'I don't know,' he shouted. 'I tell you I don't know. And if I did, I wouldn't say. Never.'

Ghote smiled, quite slowly.

'Then it is a good thing that I do know,' he said.

'You know?'

Robin's eyes flicked to and fro.

'What did she get from you?' Ghote said. 'Was it Purple Hearts? Or Black Bombers? Dexies? Bennies? Or was it the straight junk?'

The notes he had taken from a paper by a notably efficient Scotland Yard inspector at the conference had not been for nothing.

Robin thrust his little pot-belly over the counter till he was as close to Ghote as he could get.

'Listen,' he whispered hoarsely, 'I swear it wasn't the proper junk. I wouldn't give that to a kid. I can't get it anyhow. It costs money that stuff.'

Ghote put a sneer on his features.

'And of course someone like you would not get that sort of money, would they?' he said. 'So what was it you sold her? Quick.'

'It was French blues mostly,' Robin said.

Ghote absorbed this. French blues were a more recent form of the well-known Purple Hearts, an amphetamine. They got on to the market after thefts at chemists' shops.

He turned back to Robin. The tubby little man's eyes were filled with tears.

'They know I can get them,' he said, 'and they won't leave me alone till I sell them a few. But I don't let them have too many, really I don't. And they don't do anybody any harm. Medical experts tell you that. They don't do anyone any real harm.'

Ghote looked him straight between the eyes.

'Then why,' he said very quietly, 'has the Peacock been killed?'

Nine

Robin's round red face paled. It paled by stages as Ghote held him in a fixed gaze. First, all colour left the odd beaky little nose. Then the plump cheeks began to grow less and less ruddy. And finally, quite suddenly, small glistening points of sweat appeared on the forehead and it too turned like the cheeks a greyish-purple.

'I don't know about the girl being killed,' he said squeakily. 'I swear I don't know anything about that. I just saw her leave this place one night with one of the Smith Boys and I never saw her again.'

His lower lip started quivering uncontrollably and he clamped his front teeth down on it in a sharp, nervous little jab.

'The Smith Boys?' Ghote said.

'They're brothers. Three of them. They use this place.'
Robin gulped.

'I have to pay them,' he said.

With a corner of his tightly screwed-up tea-towel he began rubbing hard at one small patch of the counter.

'I have to pay, you know,' he went on. 'They came in here one day. All three of them. Jack it was who did the talking. He's the oldest. I didn't understand what he meant at first. And then I did. I had to pay up, or the place would get smashed. I told them I wouldn't. And Jack sort of nodded to Pete.'

He looked up at Ghote.

'Pete isn't quite right in the head,' he said.

His tongue shot out and licked at his upper lip.

'Well, Pete came up towards the counter. I was standing just where I am now. I thought he was going to hit me. I kept trying to make up my mind whether I'd try to call the police, or whether if I did they might find out. About my little sideline, you know. My little sideline.'

Ghote kept his features impassive.

'But Pete didn't hit me,' Robin said. 'No, he didn't hit me. He went up to the juke box instead. I kept my robin on top of it then, just like I do now.'

He glanced over at the morose, huddled bird in the bright blue cage.

'Yes,' he said, 'just as it might be now. And Pete caught hold of the cage and – and pulled the bars apart. In one go. And then he reached in and took hold of the poor birdie.'

Robin abandoned the screwed-up tea-towel and turned back to Ghote.

'He has a dog, you know,' he said. 'A black sort of a dog. And he fed my birdie to it. Fed it to his dog. So after that I had to pay.'

He looked downwards at the well-polished surface of the counter.

'And one of those three Smith brothers was attracted by the Peacock?' Ghote asked.

106

'Yes. She was in here one day, just playing the juke box. And they came in. To collect, you know. Collect their weekly cut. And Billy – that's the youngest – started chatting her up.'

The round face, slowly getting its ruddy colour back now, looked up at Ghote.

'Of course, if the girl had objected I wouldn't have stood for it. You know that. I'd have had a quiet word with young Billy. Yes, a quiet word. But she didn't object. Didn't object at all.'

He looked over towards the juke box as if re-enacting the scene in his imagination.

'Mind you,' he said, 'she didn't make a play for him or anything like that. I'll say that for her. But she was happy to let him chat her up. She was a bright kid, very bright kid. Knew all about it, she did.'

'Yes,' said Ghote.

He reflected that here was another person who had seen in the Peacock something bright and dazzling in a grey world.

'How long ago was this?' he asked.

'When she first met Billy? Oh, about six weeks ago, I'd say. Five or six weeks, if you want to put a time on it.'

He turned round and looked at a trade calendar pinned to the wall behind the chromium urn. It depicted a rum-bustious coaching scene from the proud England of long ago. Ghote found it attractive.

'Yes, five or six weeks, I'd say,' Robin concluded.

'And after that she went out with him? On many nights?'

'Oh, no, no. You got me all wrong, you have. She wouldn't really have anything to do with him. They met often enough of course. She'd be in here, laughing and joking at me to let her have a few of them pills. Only wanted 'em for a bit of a game, you know. That's why I let her have them. And Billy comes in most evenings for a bit. So he'd start larking around with her, and she'd give him back as good as she got. But when he asked her to go out with him, she'd say no. Said she'd got a boy-friend of her own and didn't want another. Quite definite on that, she was.'

'I see,' said Ghote. 'But you told me she did leave here with him once. How was that?'

'Well,' Robin said, 'she just did. He persuaded her. She kept telling him there was nothing in it for him, but he said come along all the same. And in the end she went.'

'And that was the last time you saw her?'

'I swear it was. I swear it. How was I to know the poor kid's been killed? I haven't seen nothing about it in the paper.'

'It is not certain yet she is dead,' Ghote answered. 'But she has certainly not been seen since the night of October the twenty-first last. Was that when she was in here? It was Trafalgar Day.'

Robin peered up at his coaching-scene calendar. But it omitted to record the exact dates of stirring national occasions.

He shrugged.

'Yes,' he said, 'October the twenty-first, that'd be it all right. A Friday. Yes.'

'What time did she leave with this Mr Billy Smith?' Ghote asked.

Robin puffed out his cheeks and considered.

'It was early,' he said. 'Quite earlyish. Say about seven. Yes, seven o'clock I'd say it was, give or take five minutes either side.'

'Thank you,' said Ghote. 'And now tell me, please, where does he live? Where can I find him?'

Robin's eyes seemed to bulge.

'You're not going round to the Smiths' house?' he said.

'Naturally I am. I am inquiring into the disappearance. Naturally I will have to question the person who was last seen with her on the day she disappeared.'

Again Robin pushed himself as far across the counter

108

towards Ghote as his round little stomach would allow.

'Listen,' he said, 'I never mentioned the Smith Boys' name to you. I never so much as mentioned it.'

Ghote looked at him sternly.

'You are not going to tell me where they live?' he asked.

Robin drew himself up a little. His plum-coloured waistcoat swelled.

'I don't even know,' he said. 'I don't know where they live at all.'

'You know quite well.'

But Robin's lips had set in an obstinate pout.

'Why should I know?' he said. 'Why should I know where some people who come into my café from time to time happen to live? I tell you, I just don't know.'

Ghote looked at him unblinkingly.

'You are going to tell me.'

'Certainly not.'

'Yes.'

Robin was filling his fat little lungs as if to issue another defiant 'no' when suddenly all the breath went out of him as rapidly as if he had been deflated with a pin.

His hand flew to his mouth and he sucked a little at the knuckles.

Ghote had noticed at the back of his mind that the bell on the door had pinged dully but, intent on Robin, he had paid no attention. He turned casually round now.

A big slouching dark-haired man was standing in the open doorway looking very slowly round the little café as if trying to puzzle out something unexpected. He had a heavy red complexion, further darkened by a stubble of black beard, and his mouth drooped a little bit open. He was dressed in dirty jeans, an open-necked check shirt and a heavy black leather jacket which he wore unzipped.

He stood astride, and through his legs it was possible to make out that a dog crouched behind him, a lop-sided, torn-eared black dog.

And Ghote realised whom it must be. Pete Smith. The one who had fed Robin's pet bird to his dog.

'Where's Jack? Billy?' Pete said in a slurred, difficult-to-make-out voice.

At the sound of it, Robin unexpectedly ducked down. For an instant Ghote thought he must be trying to hide, though, if so, he had certainly left it very late. But a moment later he saw him emerge through a little tunnel in the counter which he had not previously noticed.

Straightening up with a little gasp, Robin hurried over to the door.

'Not here, not here,' he said in a loud, clear voice.

He stood looking up at the huge shambling Pete from a distance of a couple of yards.

'Try somewhere else,' he said in the same loud, explaining voice. 'Try the Duke of Wellington. They often drop in there for a drink. Try the Duke.'

Pete Smith just stood looking at him, his mouth still hanging a little open.

Then suddenly he took a lumbering pace forward.

Robin darted back as if he had been about to cross a road and a fast car had come swinging round a corner. Pete's eyes lit up and he grinned. Ghote thought it was certainly not a pleasant grin.

But Robin's display of understandable fear seemed to be enough to satisfy Pete. He lurched abruptly in the other direction and slumped down on to one of the gaily painted red chairs. It creaked sharply under the impact.

'Wait,' he said in his thick, slurred voice. 'Wait here. Thass it.'

He looked cumbersomely round. His dog came slinking up and crouched at his feet.

'Tea,' he said. 'Fetch a cup o' bloody tea, Robin.'

Robin swivelled round and scuttled back through his tunnel like a plump rabbit popping into its hole. In an extremely short time he had made a cup of tea, put it on the counter, darted back out again, picked the cup up and hurried over to the table near the door.

He put the cup down in front of Pete.

'All right?' he said ingratiatingly.

Pete grunted.

Robin turned and went back towards the counter, trying hard to stick out his chest under his plum-coloured waistcoat, and not succeeding.

Pete waited until his round little bottom was just disappearing through the counter tunnel. Then he shouted.

'Juke box.'

Robin stopped as if he had come slap-up against some blank obstacle. He backed rapidly out, straightened up with a louder gasp than before and trotted over to the juke box. He pulled a coin from his trouser pocket and hastily inserted it.

With his finger hovering over the half-dozen thick white buttons on the front of the old machine, he turned to Pete.

' "It's Love, Only Love"?' he said. 'All right? It's a Johnny Bull.'

Pete grunted again.

Robin looked at him hard, trying to make out whether it had been a grunt of approval or dislike. It was plain he could not tell. In desperation he jabbed at the button under his finger.

Asthmatically the juke box began to play.

Robin looked at Pete. His big head began to nod slowly, half in time to the crude beat of the music. Robin's face took on a less anxious look. He strolled back along the counter and then made a dive for his tunnel. This time he got through unmolested.

'I think I would like another cup of coffee, please,' said Ghote.

Robin darted him a look of petulant fury. But it did not seem to occur to him that he could do anything else but reach once more for the big red tin and measure out another spoonful of powder.

Ghote watched as he held the cup under the spurting tap of the battered chromium urn. When the hissing

111

sound had stopped he offered a remark.

'I was most surprised,' he said, 'on arriving in your country to find the weather was not very cold.'

Robin straightened up from the urn.

'Oh, yes?' he said in a painfully careless conversational tone.

He brought the cup to Ghote.

'I never told you a thing,' he whispered furiously under cover of the sound of Johnny Bull's romantically yearning voice.

Ghote looked at him calmly.

'You do not need to worry,' he said quietly.

He took a sip of the coffee.

'Yes,' he said in a louder voice, 'to tell the truth I was disappointed by the weather. I was prepared to resist the intense cold, and I found there was nothing to resist.'

Robin leant a little farther towards him over the counter.

'I wouldn't speak like that if I were you,' he whispered.

He gave a tiny jerk of his head down the length of the café towards Pete.

'Doesn't much care for coloureds,' he added.

'Well, I do not want to be the cause of unpleasantness for you,' Ghote said, in a much lower voice.

Robin glanced past him towards Pete. Evidently satisfied that Ghote was grating on no sensibilities, he resumed the conversation at a discreet level well masked by the continued rhythmical pleadings of Johnny Bull issuing wheezily but loudly from the old juke box.

'Makes it a bit awkward for me at times,' he murmured. 'I do get a few Indian gentlemen in.'

He lowered his voice a little more.

'They want what I have to offer same as anybody else,' he said.

He gave Ghote a knowing little wink.

Ghote thought it best to let him go on.

'Yes,' he continued, 'a bit awkward it makes it, at times.'

Suddenly a gleam of pleasure lit up his face.

'Why,' he said, 'if you're related to a certain person, then you must be related to one of my other customers too. Stoutish gentleman, wears what you might call national costume.'

Ghote felt puzzled. Could this be Vidur Datta he was talking about? The Vidur who had sworn he had never even seen the Robin's Nest? Yet it sounded very like.

'Yes?' he said encouragingly.

'Now he's very interested in something I sometimes have for sale,' Robin said. 'Opium he cares for, opium just as it comes, you know.'

A light dawned. Vidur must be an opium-taker. That was what all the *puja* sessions would be about. A chance to take a nice relaxing dose of opium, to help stave off the impact of the Western way of life. No wonder he had been so anxious to deny knowing where the Robin's Nest was. He must, of course, take it by mouth. The smell of smoking would be too obvious. But nevertheless that was what he was. An opium-taker. An old *afim-wallah*.

The self-righteous Vidur: it was hard not to laugh.

And at that instant, by purest luck, he realised that the café door was wide open.

In the enjoyment of Cousin Vidur's unexpected discomfiture he had stopped paying proper attention to Pete Smith sitting slouched over his cup of tea by the door, and the insistent thud of Johnny Bull proclaiming 'It's Love Only Love' had blotted out entirely the clucking ping of the bell as the hulking moron had unexpectedly got up and left.

Banging down his coffee cup, Ghote turned and ran.

If he wanted to be led to the man who had last seen the Peacock alive, he must at all costs keep that man's brother in sight.

Ten

At the door of the Robin's Nest Ghote looked quickly to left and to right. There was no sign of Pete Smith or even of his slinking black dog.

Ghote's heart sank. To have got so near being led straight to the very man he wanted to see, and then at the very outset of the trail to have lost his quarry. It was almost unbearable when things were going so well.

He turned and ran quickly into the Portobello Road itself. He looked up and down the narrow street.

And Pete Smith was there, shambling along some twenty yards away. The distance was ideal on a night like this with not many people about. With a sudden flood of new confidence, Ghote buttoned up his big coat and set off in quiet pursuit.

He kept close to the inside edge of the pavement and was careful to move quickly across the shopfronts that were lit up. He soon began to feel certain that, in spite of this unfamiliar environment, he was unlikely to be spotted if Pete should happen to glance back. Often in fact he should be hardly visible in the shadows cast by the glare of the high neon signs over the occasional grocer's shop or cheap clothing store.

Pete appeared to be walking at a steady pace, keeping more or less to the middle of the pavement with his shoulders hunched and his big head down. A yard behind the black dog followed him, its belly close to the ground.

In the roadway cars swept by infrequently. The noise of their engines was almost the only sound to be heard above the constant, distant murmur of the great city itself.

Then, without any warning, from round the corner ahead there burst a group of half a dozen youngsters, sixteen or seventeen year olds, mostly wearing short, furry-collared coats over narrow trousers, and walking along shouting loudly to each other and breaking into sudden roars of pointless laughter. Within a few seconds they formed a solid screen between Ghote and his quarry.

He frowned in irritation.

The blockage would mean moving right over to the outside edge of the pavement or even into the roadway, and if Pete looked back then he might well take alarm. But there was nothing else for it. It was vital to keep him constantly in view. There could easily be odd narrow passages leading off a street like this between the old, dingy houses above the cheaply smart shops. If Pete suddenly plunged into one of these, it would be almost impossible not to lose him.

He walked rapidly out across the pavement.

'Hey.'

It was one of the noisy group. He realised that the youth who had shouted had meant it for him, but he decided to ignore him. Quickly he stepped out into the road. Pete Smith was still shambling unconcernedly along, some thirty yards ahead now.

'Hey, you. Where d'you get that coat?'

The witticism was greeted by a tremendous yell of laughter from the rest of the gang. And, without a word being said, they promptly fanned out across the road in front of Ghote till they formed a semi-circle blocking his progress.

'Excuse me,' he said. 'I am in somewhat of a hurry.'

He peered between the two tall youths nearest him. Pete's hunched back was moving steadily away.

'In somewhat of a hurry.'

Another of the boys had mimicked his accent, hitting it off to a T. He could not prevent a hot flush of shame rising to his cheeks.

''Ere,' came another voice, 'what you got under that hairy great green thing anyhow? Got a bit of cloth tucked between your legs?'

Ghote thought hard. It would be no good trying to push

115

past. That would only make them worse. And they could keep him where he was for more than long enough to let Pete get clean away.

He could turn and run. He had a notion that despite the weight of his coat he could probably outstrip his tormentors. But if he ran, he would be running in the opposite direction from Pete.

'Come on, mate, open up,' the first youth said. 'Let's see what gear they wear in the jungle then.'

And at once Ghote knew what he had to do.

Without a word, he undid the buttons of his coat from top to bottom. Then he held it wide open so that the full extent of his wardrobe could be clearly inspected.

'Do you wish me to take off my jacket?' he asked. 'And my shirt? Perhaps you would like to be sure my skin is the same colour all the way down? Should I take off my trousers?'

The gang glanced from one to the other. Nobody said anything. Not one of them looked anywhere near their victim.

And then suddenly a voice came from the edge of the group.

'Aw, let's leave 'im. It's a nutter.'

And as rapidly as they had materialised, the whole pack slipped past and went hurrying on up the street. Ten yards away they abruptly began shoving each other from side to side and whooping loudly in their relief at escaping the unnerving spectacle of the totally abject.

Ghote darted a glance ahead.

He was in luck. Pete Smith had come to a halt outside a scrubby-looking old cinema boldly labelled 'The Imperial.' He was standing gazing at the posters plastered on its front, which, even from a distance, Ghote could see advertised an action-packed Western in highly colourful terms.

He breathed a long sigh of relief and set out quietly towards the sad old building with its once proud dome outlined black against the night sky and its front, from which at some stage the heavy ornamentation had fallen away, presenting an oddly piebald appearance by the light of the street-lamps.

But before he had got as close to Pete again as he would have liked the big moron swung clumsily round, headed across the roadway heedless of an approaching vehicle and plunged into a turning opposite.

Ghote had to wait till the vehicle, a rattly old station-wagon, had gone by. He ran across the black strip of road as soon as he could, tore along to the corner and peered round.

Pete was still in sight. But now he was walking much more quickly and already he had got a great deal too far ahead for peace of mind.

The street in front was noticeably quieter than the Portobello Road itself. The houses were taller, five or six stories, and were dark and very grimy. They seemed to Ghote, walking rapidly but lightly past, to lean over towards the road with a louring solidity that houses in Bombay, no matter what the light and what the time, never came near to acquiring. For the most part there were no lights showing and the single thinly curtained windows that were lit up here and there made oblongs of glowing colour that put the rest of the background into yet deeper blackness. Many of the houses' high pillared porticoes over the steep steps leading up to their doors were badly in need of repair. Almost every wall could have done with a coat of paint many years before.

This was a new London to Ghote. It seemed far removed from the luxuries of Sloane Street and the Carlton Tower or the quiet neatness and good order of the streets round the Tagore House. It was remote too even from the comparative poverty of the tower block where Patsy and Renee lived. That, though plain, had been strikingly new and clean. Here there was only ingrained dirt and unrelieved shabbiness.

A few battered-looking cars were parked by the road-side but hardly a person was to be seen. It would be madness to break into a noisy run in the circumstances.

He hurried on at as fast a walk as he dared, keeping on the balls of his toes and leaning slightly forward as he went.

He passed a garden square on his left. But it was very different from the one near Marble Arch with its trim rectangle of lawn and elegant drooping plane trees. This was a long, broad strip of overgrown grass, tall and pale brown under the light of the street-lamps. It was entirely surrounded by a high wire-mesh fence, so that it looked almost as if it was being desperately protected against a prowling savage life outside.

Ghote shivered.

And still Pete was too far ahead. There were fewer lights now and from time to time he would be lost in an area of shadow. Ghote could hardly bear to wait for him to appear in the succeeding patch of light. Pete would only need to swing off and nip down the steps leading to the basement of one of the houses to be lost completely.

There were smaller intersecting streets too. The thought of their dangers had hardly come into Ghote's head when Pete, without slackening in his headlong pace, did wheel suddenly round and disappear from sight down one of them.

At once Ghote broke into a run. But it seemed to be an incredibly long time before he reached the corner at last and flung himself round.

The street ahead, much like the one he had been going along though narrower and even less well-lit, was com-pletely empty.

Ghote stood at the corner in utter dismay. It must not be true. Pete could not have disappeared. Yet, quite obviously, it was very possible. Although the street was not long, three other small roads led off it. Pete could have taken any one of them in the time he had been out of observation.

Ghote stared with hatred at the black length of roadway that stretched in front of him, at the empty yellow-grey pavements, at the tall dark houses, at the high, depressing red-brick wall of a school yard, at a set of distant, winking, meaningless traffic-lights.

And then he saw it.

Just at the corner of the second turning along: a little, low-bellied black dog lifting its leg against the corner wall.

A moment more and it had slunk out of sight. But Ghote knew it. Pete's dog.

He tore forward again and rounded the corner at speed, and there only fifteen yards away was Pete. Ghote teetered forward as he brought himself to a sharp halt. Then he quietly set off in pursuit once more.

Almost immediately Pete turned in at an archway between two darkened little shops. Ghote thought with a sweat of relief how completely lost he would have been if he had been out of sight a moment longer.

Quickly he walked forward. There was no knowing what might lie on the far side of the archway. There could be a number of different little alleyways. He must keep right on Pete's tail.

He nipped round into the arch, and at once almost froze with fright.

The whole entrance was cluttered with empty milk-bottles. His right foot had just tipped one of them and it was rocking like a teetotum. He remained frozen, perched over it, watching helplessly. If it should fall . . .

But at last the rocking died away. Ghote dared to look ahead. At the far end of a short length of cobbled lane, which was glistening slightly in the faint light coming from the street behind, Pete was standing at the top of a low flight of stone steps in front of a battered-looking, almost paintless door of a small, dark house. He was searching all through his pockets as if he could not find his key.

Ghote drew back a little into the corner of the side of the archway and watched.

For a few moments longer the great hulk on the steps

swore mumblingly away to himself. Then his patience appeared to give out. He grunted out a louder curse and delivered a thump on the battered surface of the door sufficient to split it in two. But nothing happened. He began thumping a tattoo which thundered and echoed round the narrow yard like cannonfire.

Ghote, looking from side to side, saw that opposite the house Pete was trying to get into there was one enormous wall with, high up in it, a line of tall windows grimly barred. He decided that it must be the back of the school he had seen earlier. On either side of the Smiths' house there were similar doors to the one Pete was attacking. But from neither of these other houses did a chink of light show and a pane in one of the ground-floor windows of the further one was gaping and broken. It looked as if the whole trio were due for demolition. London seemed to be pulsating with new building. Perhaps tall towers like Patsy's home were intended for this very spot. It was high time.

Abruptly the door on which Pete was thumping opened.

Ghote saw that a short, stout woman of sixty or so was standing there looking up at Pete with an expression of dazed pleasure on her broad, snub-nosed face across which a heavy strand of dark grey hair was trailing. She wore a huge closely-flowered apron, which covered most of her front, an enormous stretched, shapeless purple cardigan and on her bare feet a pair of bright red slippers one of which was decorated with a massive pom-pom.

'Cor,' she said in a loudly careless voice, 'you don't half make a row, Pete, when you bang on the door like that.'

Pete glowered at her.

'What you want to shut it for, Ma?' he said.

Mrs Smith burst into a wheezy, stifled laugh.

'What do I want to shut it for? It's your brothers as want it shut. It's all the same to me whether it's shut or open. So long as there's plenty of paraffin for the heaters. But they will have it shut, and you will leave it open. Oh dear, oh dear.'

She tailed away into a long outbreak of even wheezier laughter while Pete stood on the top step looking down at her.

'Well, move out of the bloody way now you are here,' he said slowly at last.

'Oh dear, oh dear, oh dear.'

Still wheezing and laughing, Mrs Smith heaved herself round and waddled off in front of her son along a narrow passage into the depths of the house.

Ghote, from his vantage point at the end of the little alley, noticed that once again Pete had left the door wide open. Evidently someone inside the house noticed it too, because a moment later there was an angry, deep-voiced yell and Pete came shambling back and banged the door closed.

The yell was very pleasing to Ghote. It must mean the two other Smith brothers were probably at home. His chance to question Billy looked as if it had come.

Taking a deep breath, he marched into the narrow unlit alley and across to the short flight of tumbledown steps. He climbed them and looked for the doorbell. All there was was a knocker, a rusty iron dolphin, forgotten reminder of a great nation's mercantile history. Ghote took hold of it but found it was too rusted to budge. Evidently visitors were unwelcome.

He doubled up his fist and banged on the old door as Pete Smith had done before him, though not with the same thunderous effect. After a little he stopped and waited.

Silence.

He was lifting his fist to try again when from the far side of the door he made out the faint sound of footsteps on bare, creaky boards.

The door opened. A young man of about twenty, with a distinct family resemblance to the moronic Pete but a great deal livelier in appearance, stood there. Behind him, shadowy in the light of a dim electric bulb, were Pete himself and another brother, older, darker and grim with suspicion, doubtless Jack, the one who had done the talking when the three of them had first asked Robin for protection money.

Looking up at Billy, Ghote saw that the tone of the encounter had to be firmly set at once or he would be met with a barrier of silence.

'Good evening,' he said cheerfully, 'is it Mr Billy Smith?'

The blackly suspicious Jack made a move in the background as if he had half a mind to stride past Billy and slam the door without a word more being said. But before he could move Billy had answered.

'That's right,' he said brightly, 'what you want?'

'You know an Indian girl they call the Peacock?' Ghote asked quickly.

Would the battered, paintless door come smashing into his face? If he had got to the heart of things, it well might.

But Billy's face retained its look of carefree inquiringness.

'Yeh,' he said. 'I know her all right. Nice kid. What about her?'

'When did you last see her please?'

''Bout three weeks ago,' Billy answered unhesitatingly. 'I been wondering where she's got to. You know her then?'

The apparent easiness of his replies posed more queries than Ghote had time to think about answering at that moment. He was tempted to explain who he was. But he decided it was important to keep up his stream of questions while Billy seemed to be willing to reply to them. He might not always be as affable as this.

'The last time you saw her,' he went rapidly on, 'whereabouts was that?'

'Met her in a place called Robin's caff,' Billy answered.

122

'Took her up West to a discothèque place.'

'And after that?'

'After that nothing, mate. I don't mind telling you it wasn't for want of trying. But I couldn't spend all night arguing, and – '

He stopped.

Behind him, somewhere in the house, a telephone bell had begun to ring shrilly. The sound surprised Ghote. It seemed odd that a tumbledown place like this should have anything like a telephone.

Billy and the others listened warily to the ringing. Then it ceased.

'Ma's there,' Billy said.

He turned his attention back to Ghote.

'What's all this about anyhow?' he said.

His eyes, for all the openness of his broad, weather-beaten face under his curly mop of dark hair, were sharp.

Ghote realised that he would have to risk giving away some of his intentions.

'It is very simple,' he said. 'This girl, the Peacock, has disappeared. It looks as if you may have been the last to see her. Can you tell me where this was?'

'It was Oxford Circus,' Billy said, hardly less cheerfully than before. 'She said she'd go home by Tube. They was still running.'

'And what was her state of mind then?'

Billy shrugged.

'Well, she was a bit sort of hoity-toity like,' he said. 'Like I told you she wasn't having any. Wouldn't even let me run her back home in the van, though I could've spared the time. She kept going on about this boy-friend, and – '

'Billy. Billy. Phone.'

It was the loud, carefree voice of Mrs Smith. Her bellow blotted out anything more Billy might have been going to say.

He turned round and yelled back.

123

'Coming.'

Pushing past his brothers he disappeared into the interior of the dark and dingy house. The two others stayed where they were, Jack eyeing Ghote with the same heavy suspicion he had shown from the outset and Pete looking at him with almost total vacancy.

Ghote hoped profoundly it would not occur to the latter to say suddenly that he had seen him before in the Robin's Nest. If Jack began to think some investigation of their activities was under way, his reaction was likely to be unpleasant. Perhaps there was something that could be done to get on his right side.

'Excuse me,' he said to him, 'were you with your brother on the evening in question?'

Jack glared at him. But eventually he muttered an answer.

'We was in the caff.'

'Ah, so you cannot much help me,' Ghote said reassuringly.

'No.'

'The girl seemed quite all right when you saw her?'

'Yeh.'

Then to Ghote's surprise Jack added a small comment.

'Yapped a lot,' he said. 'Always did, every time Billy was there.'

Ghote felt delighted. Even in this unpromising territory he was making some progress.

'And the last you yourself saw of her was in this café?' he said.

'That's right. S'pose I might've noticed her if she'd been about since. She was the kind of kid you did notice.'

Once more Ghote recorded the tribute to the Peacock's bright gaiety. It was a tribute from a source that looked sparing enough of such comments.

But now Billy reappeared. He came through a door far down along the passage and began an intense, whispered conversation with Pete. After a few moments Pete shambled down the flight of stairs Ghote could dimly make out at the end of the passage. Billy came back to the steps.

'I was just asking your brother,' Ghote said to him, 'whether the Peacock behaved quite as usual earlier in the evening of that day. He said she did.'

'Yep.'

Billy seemed less willing to talk now, and Ghote cursed the interruption for destroying the easy exchange he had managed to establish.

'Tell me,' he said quickly, 'did she ever mention Johnny Bull to you? Johnny Bull, the singer?'

'Yep.'

There could be no doubt about it: Billy was a great deal less willing to tell him anything. He decided that all he could do was to keep pegging away.

'So she did mention Johnny,' he said. 'Did she say anything particular about him?'

'He was the boy-friend.'

'Ah, yes. Thank you for telling me that. Do you happen to know him yourself?'

''Course not.'

Inwardly Ghote fumed. What on earth had Billy got into his head while he had been away? The contrast between his pleasant talkativeness before and his almost complete silence now must have some explanation.

'Did the Peacock tell you very much about Johnny?' he asked patiently.

'Not much.'

'But she told you she was in love with him?'

'Yep.'

'And did she say that he no longer – '

Suddenly from the arched entrance to the little alley there came an appalling crash. Ghote whipped round.

In the rectangle of light from the nearest street-lamp an extraordinary scene presented itself. All over the cobbled ground under the archway milk-bottles were rolling, clashing and skittering. And in the middle of them, arms flailing, legs splayed apart, body almost bent double in an effort to keep upright, was the totally inexplicable sight of Pete Smith.

Eleven

For an instant the apparition of the hulking, moronic Pete in the archway behind, when scarcely a minute before, it seemed, he had been standing with his brothers in the narrow passage of the house in front, left Ghote utterly bewildered. Then, without having time to reason it all out, he knew what had happened. Pete had been sent round a back way by Billy. And he had been sent because Billy had learnt something about him himself. Had learnt from that phone call. A call from Robin, of the Robin's Nest, of course.

In one flying bound he jumped from the top of the steps and headed hard towards the rectangle of light in the archway, the only way out of the little blind alley. If he could only get through before Pete recovered his balance, he might yet be all right.

The arch was about ten feet wide and Pete was floundering about well to the right-hand side. There should be room to shoot by.

Ghote swerved and plunged forward. All round his feet he could see the glinting, silvery shapes of the rolling bottles. He did not dare look anywhere but downwards. His feet darted and danced. The treacherous bottle swung and swivelled on every side of them.

And then the two yards of danger, which seemed interminable, were past. He was out on the pavement of the street beyond. Pete was still waving his arms and lumbering about, but that was behind him. It was even something which would serve to delay his brothers as they came after him.

Then it happened.

Pete finally and irretrievably put one of his feet fair and square on a slipping, slithering bottle. The foot shot out from under him. His whole heavy body went tumbling wildly down. And as he sprawled he just caught Ghote across the back of his legs with an almighty thwack.

Ghote fell flat on his face on to the pavement.

'Grab 'im, Pete,' yelled Billy from half-way along the alley.

Pete, slow though he was, obeyed the shouted command instantly. One great hand shot out and closed round Ghote's right thigh like the savage jaws of a mastiff.

'Bring 'im 'ere,' Billy called. 'I want a word with the bleeder.'

Pete staggered to his feet, not relaxing for a moment his iron-hard grip on Ghote's thigh. Obviously he had gathered from his brother's tone that this was someone he could treat as he liked. He strode back towards the house, holding Ghote upside down by his leg as casually as if he was carrying a wriggling dog. Ghote's head and shoulders banged and bounced on the cobbles.

He kicked out with his free leg and wriggled for all he was worth. He tried to wind his arms between Pete's feet and bring him down. But he was as powerless to hinder him as a baby.

'Bring 'im indoors,' Billy commanded.

Pete went up the broken steps two at a time. Ghote had to stop struggling completely and put his arms round his head to protect himself as best he could from the sharp edges of the stone treads.

'Now set 'im up. I got one or two things to say to 'im.'

Ghote felt himself whirled round. His face scraped the wall of the narrow passage. There was a shuddering jar through his whole frame as his feet banged on the floor, and he was staring at a furiously angry Billy straight in the face.

But Pete had not done with him yet. Pleased at his success, he began lifting him up from behind and bumping him down again on the floor with all the force of his muscular body.

Ghote thought he would lose consciousness. Every atom of breath seemed to be being jerked and forced out of him. Then at last he heard Billy speak again.

'All right, boy, leave 'im a minute. We don't want a ruddy corpse on our hands. We're deep enough in the mire already.'

With a last jarring thud Pete put Ghote down face to face with Billy for the second time, holding him helplessly pinioned.

'Right,' Billy said. 'Now just who are you working for, mate? You can't be the fuzz: we don't have no coloured cops here, thank God. So who are you with?'

'I am not with anybody,' Ghote managed to reply.

Billy bunched up a fist in front of his face.

'Now don't be bleeding stupid,' he said. 'I asked you who you were working for?'

'Please,' Ghote said, 'it is just the Peacock. She is a relation of mine. I am trying to find out what happened to her.'

'You're asking a lot of bleeding questions about us,' Billy replied contemptuously. 'And we don't like that. See?'

He held his doubled-up fist under Ghote's nose. His hand was very large.

Ghote drew a breath.

'If you did no harm to the Peacock,' he said, 'you have nothing to fear.'

'I've got nothing to fear?' Billy answered. 'It's you who've got something to fear, matey. Plenty to fear.'

He took a pace backwards in the narrow passage and drew back his fist.

'Now,' he said, 'are you going to get out and keep out, or am I going to bash your stupid head in?'

Ghote looked at him dazedly. He had to go on with his investigation. He was a police officer. He had set an inquiry on foot. He could not allow threats to his personal safety to halt it.

And yet he knew at the same time, with dismal certainty, that he had let himself get caught. He had got himself into a situation he could not get out of. And there would be a limit to the amount of punishment he could take. If he refused to back down and the burly figure looking at him so intently at this moment began using that great doubled-up fist, there would come a time sooner or later when he would cry out. Cry out for mercy.

Why not give in now?

And betray himself as a policeman? Betray himself as an Indian even? 'We don't have no coloured cops here, thank God.' Billy's words were there to taunt him.

He knew that he should force his head up, look his tormentor straight in the eye and throw at him some challenging question. Where is the Peacock?

'You won't speak, eh?' said Billy with open savagery. 'Right.'

He poised himself.

'No,' said Ghote. 'No, stop.'

And then, there was another voice.

'Now then, what's all this?'

It was an unmistakable voice. The calm, authoritative tones of the police constable.

The moronic Pete dropped Ghote like a trained dog caught with its master's dinner in its mouth. He shambled round to stare out into the alley. Ghote, putting out a hand to the grimily papered wall for support, also turned. Behind him Billy and Jack moved first a quick step back and then more slowly and brazenly half a step forward.

Beyond the door of the house, which Pete had as usual left open, the constable could be seen standing at the foot of the broken-edged steps looking up at them. The light coming through the archway illuminated one side of his helmet, glinted on its black strap as it lay along the stern line of his jaw, glistened and gleamed on his cape. His feet were firmly planted in heavy boots on the cobbles, his look was mildly disapproving.

And abruptly Ghote felt an overwhelming tidal wave of sheer embarrassment. He had just at that moment betrayed himself. He had surrendered, surrendered abjectly to the threat of force. And it was as if the heavens had at once moved majestically apart so that his act of cowardice could be seen in its full baseness.

He could not bring himself to speak.

The Smith brothers seemed equally disinclined to say anything.

But the silence in no way disturbed the constable. He waited patiently for some time, and then supplied an answer to his own question.

'Having a bit of what you'd call fun, I dare say,' he pronounced, looking sternly from brother to brother.

Pete, more suggestible that the others, grinned uneasily.

'Right then,' the constable said impassively, 'now don't let's be hearing any more of this. You're in trouble enough already, the three of you, without adding to it.'

He pursed his lips firmly.

Then he turned to Ghote.

'You'd better come along now,' he said.

He moved a little as if to usher Ghote down. Silently Ghote came forward past the cowed-looking Pete, descended the flight of broken steps and turned towards the rectangle of light in the alley archway.

The constable paced solemnly behind him. At the arch he swung round.

'You lads better get these bottles cleared up,' he said. 'If it hadn't been for all that noise just now I might never have come along. And then where would you have been.'

130

Without waiting to see if his instructions were going to be obeyed, he moved calmly away. Ghote found it necessary to trot a little to keep beside him.

For some time they walked along together without a word being spoken. But at last the constable turned to Ghote.

'Well now,' he said, 'and what was all that about?'

'I am afraid I was very stupid,' Ghote began.

'Ah, well, we can't all expect to be right all of the time. Specially when we're not in our proper part of the world as it were.'

The contrast between the constable's authoritative handling of the Smiths and his own appalling display was too vivid in Ghote's mind for him to accept this as a universal truth. He could not but feel that wherever in the world the constable might find himself he would behave with exactly the same totally convinced calm.

But he was not doing anything about explaining the situation. He started off anew.

'I am a policeman also, however,' he said to the stately figure at his side. 'I am an inspector in the Bombay C.I.D.'

'Very nice, I'm sure.'

The constable contented himself with this single observation and, after pacing along for some time in silence, Ghote was forced to pick up his explanation where he had left it off.

'All the same,' he said a little lamely, 'you will be wondering what I was doing conducting an investigation here in London.'

'Conducting an investigation, were you, sir?' the constable said placidly.

Ghote felt a new flush of hot shame.

'But I was on unfamiliar ground,' he said. 'I should have known better. That is what I have been telling you. I let myself get into that most awkward situation. It was the height of stupidity.'

'It wasn't very sensible, certainly,' the constable agreed gravely.

'You know those men, it seemed,' Ghote said.

'Oh yes, sir. Know 'em well. They're the stars of my particular patch as you might say. As nasty a bunch as you'll get.'

There was an unmistakable note of pride in the declaration.

'Yes, I suspected they were a pretty bad lot,' Ghote said. 'Tell me, do you think they would go as far as murder?'

The constable gave a warm chuckle.

'Well, all I can say is: they haven't yet.'

'But you think they would be capable of it?' Ghote asked with sharpness.

They had come to the corner of a broad well-lit thoroughfare. The constable halted his ponderous march. He stood looking down at Ghote.

'Now, sir,' he said, 'I think we'll put all that sort of thing out of our minds, shall we? You got yourself a nasty fright there, but it's all done with now.'

The constable looked round about him.

'Now, whereabout is it you live, sir?' he asked.

'I am staying with relatives in Hyde Park Terrace,' Ghote answered impatiently. 'But I am anxious to know more about these men. It's a piece of luck meeting someone who probably knows as much about them as anybody.'

'I dare say I do that,' the constable replied.

'Well then, how much trust can I put in any of their statements? I ask because there is a young girl, the niece of the people I am staying with, who has disappeared. And I have reason to believe she was last seen alive in the company of Mr Billy Smith.'

The constable raised his eyebrows gravely.

'A missing girl now, is it, sir?'

'Yes, yes. So, you see, it is import–'

132

'Excuse me, sir, but has this matter been reported to your local police-station?'

'Yes, yes. Of course. But –'

'It has, has it? And they made a full note of all particulars?'

'Yes, certainly. I went there myself to check.'

'Very sensible of you, I'm sure, sir. And now –'

Ghote interrupted.

'But that is not the point,' he said energetically. 'You see, I have since made inquiries of my own, and I have discovered certain matters that put the case in a totally new light.'

'Yes, sir? Well, let me give you a little piece of advice.'

The constable looked at him severely.

'I think you'll find, sir, that if the local police-station has been informed that a person is missing it'll be best, by and large, to leave the whole matter to them. They'll do everything that should be done.'

'Yes, yes. But it so happens that in this case I have discovered extra particulars.'

Ghote looked up at the constable who was now blandly regarding the night-time scene.

'I was following up the particulars in question when you came upon me just now,' he added.

'Ah,' said the constable, 'so that's what it was.'

And, before Ghote could say another word, he gestured gravely along the road.

'There's a Number 15 bus just coming along, sir,' he said. 'It'll take you right to Marble Arch. Can you find your own way home from there?'

'Yes, of course I can. But you do not seem to realise –'

'You have got money for the fare, sir?'

'Constable, I am telling you the Smith brothers may be implicated in a most serious matter.'

'They're as implicated as they can get already, sir,' the constable said. 'But if you miss this bus we may have to wait a fair time for the next one. The service is none too good at this time of night. And I've got plenty to be seeing to.'

Gently gripping Ghote by the elbow, he propelled him, smoothly as a rubber-wheeled trolley, in the direction of the bus-stop a few yards away. The Number 15 was at that moment drawing up.

'There we are, sir,' the constable said.

He helped Ghote up on to the platform of the bus. Ghote angrily shook his hand off. The constable seemed utterly undisconcerted.

'One last little tip, sir, if you won't take it badly,' he said. 'A foreign gentleman like yourself shouldn't really go wandering about after dark, not unless he keeps to the well-lighted streets, sir.'

'Hold very tightly please.'

It was the West Indian conductor.

He grinned cheerfully at Ghote and at the constable and pinged merrily on his starting-bell. With one slight lurch, the bus moved relentlessly away.

Ghote's rage did not really come to a head till next morning. By the time he had got back to the Tagore House after being put on the bus he had been so dispirited that he had had only one concern: to reach the safety of his bed without encountering Cousin Vidur or, worse, Mrs Datta.

By creeping up the very edge of the stairs and swinging past the door of the sitting-room, with one foot close to the base of the banisters and a hand on the newel-post, he had contrived this. He had just enough energy left to examine himself to see what harm Pete had inflicted and to discover that, thanks mostly to the thickness of his coat, he had in fact got off with no more than minor scrapes on his hands. And then he had tumbled into bed and fallen into a deep sleep.

But with the new day the events of the past evening presented themselves with well-ordered, unpleasant clarity. And first and foremost in his mind was a feeling of passionate fury over the way his rescuer had treated him. It outweighed even his sense of shame at his own behaviour at the hands of the Smith brothers.

How very different the constable had turned out to be from what he had at first seemed. Appearing in that god-like way at the moment of his worst humiliation, he had seemed to be the ideal British policeman, a figure like the one he had seen with such delight at London Airport. But in fact he had turned out to be far worse than the unhelpful sergeant at the local police-station. That someone as pompous, self-satisfied and prejudiced could be walking the beat as a London policeman sent all his notions of what Britain stood for cascading to pieces.

A little later, sitting in the Tube train cutting along under the ground from Marble Arch to the Bank, he found he was giving the stolid Englishmen sitting opposite a prolonged glare of shocked indignation. It was lucky, indeed, that they were Englishmen and were far away in their morning papers or staring stonily in front of them as oblivious as possible of any other human being.

The sight of them at least served to channel his rage of disillusion.

He would not just sit and glower. He would do something.

And luckily he was in a position to do that something, if ever anyone was. After all, he was on his way to a day's sessions of the Conference on the Smuggling of Dangerous Drugs. And dangerous drugs plainly lay at the heart of the business of the Peacock's disappearance. That was the very point he had been trying to make to that stupid constable.

All right, he had failed with him: he would succeed with someone a good deal higher up the scale than a constable. And one happy side-effect of that would be a pretty sharp reprimand for a certain exceptionally stupid and obstinate policeman.

He thought more coolly. Yes, he knew the man to see.

A detective-inspector who had delivered early on in the conference the particularly impressive paper on the present state of the drugs racket in London, the paper from which he had culled the inside knowledge that had enabled him to get some answers out of the evasive Robin.

It would be much better to consult someone like this than to go to Superintendent Smart. The man with the fewer responsibilities, that was the one to go for.

First, he would tell him about Robin and his Nest as a newly-discovered centre of drug distribution, and then he would go on to say how this had come to light through Johnny Bull. To think that drugs from his own Bombay were being hawked about so blatantly that even someone like Johnny Bull knew at once where they could be picked up.

He began to make a careful arrangement in his mind of the main heads of the verbal report he would present as soon as the day's proceedings were over and he could get his chosen inspector aside for a reasonable length of time.

In comparison with the day before when time for Ghote, eager to make his way to the Robin's Nest, had seemed to creep by to-day it flew. His notebook almost filled itself with useful and concise observations, and then to a dutiful patter of applause the last speaker of the day brought his paper to a conclusion.

Ghote jumped up and walked rapidly over to the heavy ornamental doors of the hall before any of the other delegates had had time to leave. And all was set: he had only to wait till his man came in sight.

Soon enough he did so. Ghote stepped forward.

'Inspector,' he said, 'might I have a word with you?'

The inspector looked at him. He was a tall, gaunt-faced man with a stiff crown of short black hair and a bar of black moustache all across his upper lip. Though from the Metropolitan Force, he had delivered the paper that had so impressed Ghote in what had sounded like a Scottish accent, dry and purposeful.

'Inspector Ghote, isn't it, of Bombay?'

Ghote felt it was typical of the man's efficiency that he should know his name when they had barely been introduced.

'Yes, yes,' he said. 'Ghote. Ghote is my name. I am here in place of Superintendent Ketkar, after his most unfortunate accident.'

'Yes, yes. There was something particular you wanted to see me about?'

'There is, Inspector. Something that I think will bring you a certain amount of pleasure.'

'Indeed?'

The black bar of moustache chopped down on the word like a moving part in some relentlessly efficient machine.

Ghote coughed. Once.

'Inspector,' he said, 'for reasons I will not immediately enter into, it has so happened that during my stay in London I have felt bound to make certain investigations. And during the course of my inquiries I had occasion to visit a certain café-establishment a few yards off the Portobello Road, W.11.'

He looked up at his companion. He felt he was producing his facts with exemplary precision, and was anxious to detect any answering flicker. But the thin lips beneath the thick black bar of moustache were unmoving.

He went on.

'The name of the establishment in question is the Robin's Nest. And in the course of my investigation there and elsewhere I discovered – '

'That the good Robin pushes whatever dope he can lay his little paws upon.'

The words were spoken sharply in that particularly cutting Scots accent.

Ghote blinked.

'Thank you for your information, Inspector,' the Scots-

man said. 'And now let me tell you something: your friend
Robin continues his activities only just so long as we think
he'll lead us to someone worth occupying our time about,
and not one moment longer.'

The thin lips twisted in a sudden spasm of pent-up
irritation.

'And I hope to hell, Inspector, that nothing you've seen
fit to do has alerted that particular gentleman.'

Ghote sought wildly for something to answer.

The Scotsman gave him a last furious glare.

'And now, if you'll excuse me, I'll say good day. I
happen to have a considerable amount of work to do.'

He turned on his heel and left Ghote standing rooted to
the gleamingly polished parquet floor of the lofty, dignified, quietly magnificent conference hall.

Twelve

The last of the conference delegates, anxious to go about
their business of the evening, poured past Ghote on their
way out through the wide-flung doors under their stately
surround of heavy wood. Occasionally one of the more
eager or less observant than the others, jostled him. But
he continued to stand on the very spot where he had been
when the Scots inspector left, like a post jutting up in
some fast-flowing stream, its weedy covering just touched
by the rush of water but itself totally unmoving.

The thoughts went tumbling through his head.

So the news he had been so proud to be bringing to his
British colleague for the great campaign against crime
wherever it reared its head was no news at all. The telling
of it had even put into his colleague's head the notion that
he himself had bungled about like a real amateur and

spoilt some carefully-laid plan.

And there had not even been time enough for him to give an assurance that this had not been so. His whole well-thought-out recital had been cut short at the outset. He had had no opportunity even of making the point that this traffic in drugs from his own Bombay was so well-established that even a person like Johnny Bull knew just where they were to be bought.

Let alone had there been a chance to make any incidental remarks about a certain officious police constable.

And, through all this, shot the thought that he had been treated with the minimum of consideration by the very man he had selected to be his informant. He had hardly even been granted courtesy. Everything his racing mind turned to was lit up and distorted by the biliously yellow light this cast.

It was the final humiliation. He had thought his investigation was going so well. And then, one after another, had come these black defeats – the rough handling by the three brothers, rescue in circumstances even more humiliating, and now this final snub from a colleague at the conference, the very conference which had all along given him that comfortable feeling of status.

He would give up the whole business.

Yes, that was it. Throw in his hand. Why not? He had done his best. He had done more, much more, than could reasonably have been expected of him. And he had met with this final, miserable rebuff. All right. That would be that. He would give up.

A doubt struck him.

Could he give up as easily as all that? Wouldn't Cousin Vidur and Mrs Datta have something to say? Hadn't they after all succeeded in setting him on?

And almost in the same instant he realised that he had got the perfect answer.

He was in a position to make his own terms with the Dattas. He had at least learnt one useful thing in the course of last night. He had learnt that the stately, self-opinionated Vidur was nothing but a sneaking old *afim-wallah*.

Suddenly he felt a gleam of pleasure, such as he had hardly expected to feel again in the whole course of his stay. Now he knew why all those bottles and packets and jars of laxatives were ranged on the Dattas' mantelpiece: constipation was the classic side-effect of opium-eating.

He smiled to himself.

At least it should not be very difficult to see, if necessary, that Cousin Vidur took his side in any dispute about continuing the case. And Cousin Vidur would just have to lay down the law to his wife, a pastime he generally seemed pleased enough to do in any case.

Things at once began taking on a rosier hue. Freed of the burden of his investigation, he would have time to enjoy his visit. He could see all those sights – the Tower, the Houses of Parliament, the Old Bailey. And he would have plenty of time to deal with the neglected question of the present for Protima. All that that needed was sufficient opportunity to look around at things for himself. And now he would have it.

He glanced round, astonished that the lofty, high-windowed, airy hall behind him should already be empty of people, and hurried off to the now familiar Tube station.

But, when he got back to the Tagore House and began to break the news of his intention of releasing himself from the burden which Cousin Vidur and Mrs Datta had combined to place on him, he found that after all things were not going to go as he had planned.

He had had an unexpectedly chilly walk from the Tube at Marble Arch, thanks to the sudden upspringing of a hard cold wind which whipped levelly along the streets sending an occasional crinkled dried leaf skittering wildly along the bare pavement.

He hung up his big coat on one of the downstairs pegs, grateful for almost the first time for the garment's heavy warmth. He then marched resolutely up to the sitting-room, hoping to find both the Dattas there together so that the business he had set his hand to could be dealt with at one clean blow. And surely enough, both Cousin Vidur, standing in front of the little popping gas fire, sturdy legs apart, and his wife, sitting on the edge of one of the low couches with a purple piece of knitting in her hands, were there seemingly almost too ready to hear what he had to say.

'Ah, Cousin, Cousin,' Vidur began, giving Ghote a look of keen interest, 'and how is it going, your search for our lost girl?'

Ghote darted him a quick glance. As he had expected, there plain to see if they were looked for were the typical pin-pointed pupils of the opium-taker. It was pleasant to note their existence. They were an insurance. If the coming conversation did not go just as he wanted it to, he could take Cousin Vidur on one side and put certain matters to him. After which he would have no more trouble.

So he replied cheerfully enough.

'Well, Cousin,' he said, 'up to a point things have been going well. I have some information for you which I know you will be able to make use of yourselves. But I regret to say that, as for me, I shall not be able to go on with the inquiry.'

It was then that Mrs Datta put her question.

She looked up from the slowly descending oblong of deep purple that was her knitting and, with the steel spectacles glued to her face a little more askew than usual, she gave him a single direct look.

'But have you no pride in finishing the job you have begun?' she said.

And, to his own considerable astonishment, Ghote found that there could be only one answer: he had indeed

141

too much pride to quit. Seen in this light, there was no possible way out.

'Pride?' he stammered. 'But – Well – Well, I know what you mean. That is to say, I have not completely given up, not completely.'

Then he produced for them both a short résumé of his work the evening before. He concluded by describing, briefly, the attack the Smith brothers had made on him. But he did not say what had happened after 'a passing constable in the nick of time happened to see what was going on and came to the rescue.'

During his recital Mrs Datta had gone back to her knitting, with a steady click of needle on needle which Ghote had found obscurely irritating. At the end of it, without ceasing to move the prominent knuckles of her hands in the same vigorous rhythm, she made one comment.

'That man Robin: he is the one.'

'What do you mean?' Ghote snapped at her.

'The man Robin is the one who is hiding my Peacock.'

Ghote went over and sat seriously beside her.

'I am afraid I have bad news,' he said.

'You have more to tell?'

'No, nothing more. But it seems you have not drawn the right conclusions from what I have said.'

Mrs Datta brought her lips together in a hard-drawn knot of disbelief. But she said nothing.

'I am afraid,' Ghote continued soberly, 'that I have been forced to the conclusion that almost certainly the Peacock is no longer alive.'

But it was plain that Mrs Datta had not really been listening. She had been prepared for politeness' sake to pretend to give him her attention, but as soon as that charade was over her eyes glinted with purpose once again.

'Yes,' she said. 'And now I will order them in the kitchens to bring you a good meal, and then you can go to the Robin's Nest and find where he is keeping her.'

Ghote tried once more.

'Police work is largely a matter of experience,' he observed as a beginning.

'Yes, yes,' Mrs Datta agreed vigorously. 'It is good that you have plenty of experience. You will know what to say to this Robin. You will know what will make him give her up.'

'But that is not the question.'

Mrs Datta turned round on the edge of the couch and stopped her knitting. She looked Ghote fair and squarely in the eyes through her glinting spectacles.

'It is the question,' she said. 'Otherwise I would go round and deal with him myself.'

And at this the barriers broke and a fountain of pent-up rage swooshed up in Ghote's head.

'It is not the question, not the question at all,' he shouted. 'The question is: how am I going to find out what the Smith brothers know when they have threatened to knock me senseless if I go anywhere near them. And they can do it.'

He sat and glowered at Mrs Datta.

'You should not go to the Smith brothers,' she replied with calm.

For a moment Ghote thought she was allowing him to back out. He did not know whether he was still prepared to, but the feeling that the opportunity was there opened new prospects to him. But then he realised, with the inevitability of all good anti-climaxes, that all she was saying was that he ought to be going to the Robin's Nest instead of the Smiths' house.

He jumped up.

'A meal can wait,' he said. 'I am going round there now. To the Smiths'. You understand? To the Smiths'. To the Smiths'.'

Ghote made his way on foot to the dingy tumbledown

area where the Smiths' house was situated. He had felt altogether too enraged to wait tamely for a Number 15 bus to take him sedately to his destination. And, after having marched angrily through the wind-whipped streets of Bayswater for about a mile, he found in any case that he had come to the conclusion he ought to think things over very carefully before he actually got to the house itself.

So for the remainder of the journey – it was perhaps a couple of miles all told – he walked along more quietly, turning over in his mind the various possibilities. And, well before he had reached his destination, he had formulated a plan.

Plainly, the thing to do was simply to lie in wait at some convenient point near the house and keep watch until he had made sure all three of the brothers had gone out. From all he had heard, it was clear that they were out of the house often enough – either at the Robin's Nest drinking cups of tea and playing the juke box at little Robin's expense, or in the Duke of Wellington public-house or presumably in other places. But their sprawling, loud-voiced mother, on the other hand, looked as if she seldom got out of her soft slippers and vast flowered apron to go trundling round the neighbourhood.

And with her sons out of the way, it might be possible to get something out of her. The only snag was that counting the three brothers out was not going to be all that simple.

Pete had after all suddenly appeared in the entrance to the alley the night before when a few minutes earlier he had been standing indoors. A careful exploration of the immediate neighbourhood of the crumbling old house was called for.

Coming down the street where he had thought he had finally lost Pete in the chase from the Robin's Nest, Ghote began looking about him to get a more accurate picture of the lie of the land.

And then suddenly, unmistakably, he saw the constable, his rescuer. Walking towards him from the far end of the road, with that leisurely, proprietorial air he had studied the evening before, was the very same man.

Like a little furry animal darting into the safety of its hole, Ghote simply nipped round the nearest corner and broke into an undignified sprint. This was an encounter he would not face, come what might. To be taken solemnly to task for disobeying the sage advice he had been given as he was put on that Number 15 bus: that would be altogether too much to endure, summon up his patience how he might.

He slowed down and came to a stop.

But, if the fellow was on the beat in the neighbourhood, at any moment he might be surprised by him.

He turned and cautiously made his way back to the point where he had taken flight. He peered carefully round the corner, and, with a small feeling of satisfaction, located his rescuer once more. He was standing by the turning of the street where the alley leading to the Smiths' house was. And, as Ghote watched, he seemed to make up his mind and moved ponderously off.

Quickly Ghote followed. He was in good time to see him taking up, with due deliberation, a station in a dark shop doorway about thirty yards away from the alley entrance and on the opposite side of the road.

So they had both decided to spy on the Smiths.

Ghote came to the conclusion that this suited him very well. If the constable was going to stay where he was for a little, he himself could find out undisturbed just how it was that Pete Smith had taken him in the rear the evening before.

And, without much trouble, he quickly enough hit on what looked as if it might be the answer. There seemed to be no back alley leading to the Smiths' house, but almost at once he found between the nearest street and the house a long, single-storey building which looked as if it ought not to be too much of an obstacle. It was a small factory, blank and shuttered, with a single drab painted signboard fixed to the wall saying 'Easifoam Products Ltd.' in yellow letters on a green background. It had a grey-slated, gently-sloping roof.

Ghote inspected it more closely. And at one end he found there was a narrow niche about three feet deep between the factory itself and the house next door. And at the back of this niche a solid-looking drainpipe ran up to a long gutter.

There would be no difficulty in shinning up, sheltered from any passer-by in the niche. Getting across the gentle slope of the roof would present no problem. But what lay on the other side? How quickly could someone complete the journey from the house?

Ghote stepped out into the road and looked up and down it. No one in sight. For a cautious minute or two he stood pretending to stare up at the factory noticeboard in an interested manner. He even actually found himself wondering about the difference in English and Indian law that decreed that while at home the name of the factory would probably have been Easifoam Products (Private) Ltd. here it was only Easifoam Products Ltd.

Shaking his head to clear away such idle thoughts, he took a last quick glance at the empty street, darted into the niche, grasped the drainpipe and heaved himself upwards.

Five seconds later he was at roof level. Moving on all fours like a monkey, he clambered rapidly over the slates to the top and then down the gentle slope on the far side till he was certain he would be safe from observation from the road.

He paused to look round.

On this side of the factory there were two concrete yards, similar expanses of bare cement, one with a few oil drums stacked together in the middle and the other with a small pile of cardboard containers. They were separated by a high wall. Each of them was lit brightly and barely by an outside light from the factory itself, one protected by a thick glass cover, the other with its cover dangling loose.

To get down into either one of them would be comparatively easy. It would mean shuffling along the gutter on this side and dropping down about twelve feet. But it would be a pointless operation: once down, there was no way up on the far side from either one yard or the other.

Ghote looked out into the darkness. The bleak-looking back of a tall house which might well be the Smiths' was not far away. In two of its windows lights shone. One was curtained and glowed a bright yellow. Through the other a glimpse of some pallid green wallpaper and the edge of a brown cupboard could be seen.

Then, as he watched, the unmistakable sprawling silhouette of Ma Smith appeared in the second window. It was there only for an instant, but that was long enough.

Ghote surveyed the space between his perch on the roof and the lighted windows with new care. And then he saw how it might be that Pete had got out. To drop down into either of the two yards directly in front of him was to be trapped, but between them there was a straight path leading right to the Smiths' backyard: the top of the dividing wall.

The wall looked well-built, a craftsman's job such as he would have expected in England. It was high, but the top was a good nine inches wide, neatly and smoothly made with a little ledge jutting out on each side about three inches down. Given a cool head, there would be no difficulty in traversing the twenty feet or so from this end to the Smiths' yard. And if at that end there was some convenient way down, then he would know just how Pete got in and out and could safely keep watch solely on the front entrance. A route such as this would be for emergency use only.

Ghote wriggled down on to the top of the high wall and set out. His bulky overcoat was a bit of an encumbrance, and he was glad that the wind here was less strong than in the street. But he made good progress, arms held out to

147

either side for balance. Ten feet, fifteen.

And he was there. He peered downwards. Yes, it was the backyard of the Smiths' house itself. And there, rising out of a great deal of cluttered mess, was a substantial concrete coal bunker with the lid half-off. It formed an ideal stepping-stone up to the top of the wall.

This was all he needed to know. He manœuvred himself back round.

And then, quite distinctly in the comparative quiet, he heard a noise he immediately recognised. It was the sound of someone else clambering laboriously up the slates on the far side of the factory roof.

One of the brothers coming back this way: it could be nothing else. They had spotted the constable watching the alley entrance and had decided to come in unobserved.

What should he do?

He swung round and peered again at the half-lit gloom of the Smiths' yard. But it would be asking for trouble to try and hide in the clutter there: he was almost bound to knock into something and then the brothers would be on to him in a flash.

He turned back again. In a few seconds he would be plainly visible to anyone coming over the top of the roof.

Should he drop down into one of the factory yards? But they were bare and mercilessly lit.

Then he saw what he could do. Recklessly he bounded back along the narrow top of the wall till he was almost at the factory end. Then, just where the twin yard-lights were fixed high up on the factory wall, he stooped, hung his legs down and kicked out viciously.

To his infinite relief he hit the yard-light which had lost its thick protective cover first time. He looked down into its yard. It was now a deep pool of blackness, all the more inky because of its brightly lit companion yard next door.

He swung himself down from the top of the wall on that side. If only whoever it was coming over the roof was not in too much of a hurry.

148

Clinging to the top of the wall, he lowered his left hand cautiously. The little ledge three inches from the top felt firm and secure. He lowered his right hand to it.

It was a wrenching strain, but he was able to hang there safely enough, the tips of his fingers clasping hard at the little ledge and his body pressed to the dirty yellow brick of the wall below.

In the dark and silence he waited.

Within a few moments he heard the slither of someone heavy coming down the roof. There was a grunt as the top of the wall was reached. He held his breath.

It was impossible to be certain about the sounds from directly above. Whichever brother it was who was coming along the wall was wearing rubber-soled shoes. He waited and waited. Would they glance straight down and be able to make out the top of his head? Or was the yard so dark that it really would blot him out completely?

Then suddenly he heard the sound of a quiet belch. It came from directly above him.

He counted the seconds. Ten. Twenty. And then came the wonderful sound of a heavy thump from the far end of the wall. Plainly someone jumping down on to the coal bunker.

He forced himself to stay hanging there for a carefully counted spell of exactly five minutes. Then he began hauling himself up. The moment at which the weight came off his right hand was wonderful. In the spasm of relief it brought he almost lost his grip. But he flailed out wildly and safely caught the top of the wall on the far side. He scrabbled at the brickwork with his toes.

And there he was. Back crouching on the wall once more. He stayed where he was, exhausted and trembling.

Then without warning a door in the Smiths' backyard was jerked open. His heart went into his mouth. He could not move. He could not go down and hang there again.

There was the sound of an empty can clonking out into the yard and the door was slammed shut. Ghote found the relief gave him a new spring of energy. He scuttled up the low slope of the roof in seconds and slithered down on the other side.

He took a quick glance at the street. No one was about. He breathed a deep sigh. To be down on the ground once more and to be able to pass as someone going about their proper business, it would be as comforting as being at home.

He shifted himself into position to swing over and slip down the drainpipe.

And then he saw, just below him in the narrow niche itself, a tiny glow of light.

Thirteen

Peering down into the darkness as he lay flat on the slight slope of the factory roof, Ghote realised at once that the source of the tiny unexpected glow of light below was a cigarette. But there was still something puzzling about it, or about the vague outline of a face which it illuminated.

Then, like a piece from a jigsaw suddenly turned round, he saw what it was he had been staring at: the top of a policeman's helmet. He peered harder and saw that, as he had half-known he would, it was none other than his mentor who was standing there.

He supposed that policemen in London were forbidden to smoke on the beat. And no doubt occasionally they succumbed to the temptation. Even the most majestic of them.

Patiently Ghote settled down to wait on the wind-lacerated roof. It occurred to him to wonder just what it was that was made in the little factory below. Easifoam Products. They sounded somehow so much what ought to be made in the contemporary Britain he was beginning to discover that, looking at the signboard earlier on, he had never even thought to ask himself exactly what sort of products they were.

He lay and puzzled about it for some time. But he had hit on no satisfactory answer when quite suddenly the constable below ground the butt of his cigarette under his boot and moved dignifiedly off. Ghote was able to hear his measured steps all the way along the street till they rounded the far corner. Immediately he swung down on to the drainpipe and an instant later was on the ground.

Without weighing the pros and cons, he headed simply for the familiar bus-stop. He had had enough for one night. And, as one of the brothers had taken so much trouble to get home unobserved, it was hardly likely he would go out again in a hurry.

Besides there was the conference again next day. His notes must be as full and precise as ever.

But, sitting on his smart black leather chair at Wood Street police-station next morning, Ghote found that it was much harder than he had expected to give his full attention to the papers that were read and the subsequent questions and discussion. The thought of the Smiths' house kept swimming into his mind and threatening to overwhelm everything else.

He was relieved that, being a Saturday, there were to be papers in the morning only. The afternoon was to be given over to an outing, a tour of the newest of the various buildings that have housed Scotland Yard. And, much though he would have liked to have gone on this, he had earlier refrained from booking himself a place. There was not going to be time during his stay for anything that smacked remotely of frivolity. He had realised that days ago.

But at length the session drew to an end. As it did so, Ghote's impatience mounted.

What is happening at the house now? Has anybody gone out yet? Are the brothers the sort to be up and about early? What about old Ma Smith, does she go shopping on Saturday afternoons? The questions popped up one after another.

And then he was free. He almost ran to the big double-doors, pushing past the more staid of his colleagues already beginning to relax after their hard work of the past few days.

'Inspector Ghote. Inspector Ghote.'

He realised that someone was calling his name in a high, clear sharp voice. Could he ignore it? Too many people knew him by sight now and someone was bound to stop him. Probably he was wanted to be told when he was to read his own, or rather Superintendent Ketkar's, paper. It had been a prospect he had deliberately put out of his mind. With a feeling of hot trepidation, he turned round.

And, making his way directly towards him, was Superintendent Smart.

Ghote's heart began suddenly to race.

How could he, he asked himself, have mistaken one of the world's leading authorities on narcotics crime for a detective-sergeant on the verge of retirement? He had even called him 'Sergeant.' He had leant out of the police car and said 'Thank you, Sergeant.'

Yet somehow the figure advancing towards him still did not look as he ought to have done, in spite of the dark blue suit with the chalk-stripe which had replaced the dirtyish trench-coat and the woollen gloves. Perhaps it was the fact that the suit looked a little too big and a little too stiff so that its occupant still had something about him of the circumspect tortoise. Or perhaps it was the way in which his rather faded quietly striped tie was tucked so resolutely away into the waistcoat under the stiff collar of the white shirt.

Whatever it was, Ghote thought as he watched like a

hypnotised rabbit the approach of the man he had insulted, there was after all some justification for his mistake. But how on earth could he refer to it in the apology he must make?

It took Smart of the Yard an incredibly long time, it seemed, to weave his way through the milling delegates and at last to reach his target. When he had done so he manœuvred himself right up close to Ghote amid the cheerful buzz of conversation all around before he spoke.

Then suddenly his warily anxious face lit up in the notably sweet smile Ghote remembered.

'My dear chap,' he said, 'you must forgive me, I've been trying to say hallo ever since the conference began, and I just never seemed to see you.'

Approaching the neighbourhood of the Smiths' house about an hour after his encounter with Superintendent Smart, Ghote found himself possessed of a new, quiet confidence about the prospect before him. Somehow their ten minutes of friendly and mild exchanges on the differences between life in London and life in Bombay had given him an altered outlook on everything he came into contact with. Their comparisons of the noise of the traffic in each city, the pressures of the crowds, the punctuality of the transport services – Ghote had insisted that here London must and should take the palm – had infused in him a new way of looking at things. Under it even the incident of his rescue at the hands of the ponderous constable, which the sight of a Number 15 bus reminded him of at that very moment, appeared in a changed light.

After all, he thought, if the top positions in the Metropolitan Police were occupied by men like Superintendent Smart, people of such serene modesty and simple strength of character, then the way that a man in the lowest rank happened to behave was unimportant.

The very existence indeed of someone in Smart's position who could cheerfully forgive the sort of slight that he had put on him – and there could be no doubt that the slight had been noticed when Smart for all the quietness of his manner was plainly a man of such shrewdness – gave Ghote a more optimistic outlook on every venture the human race could undertake, whether it might be the urging of a great nation through the stormy seas of time, or a mere attempt to penetrate the secrets of a gang of petty protection racketeers.

He made his approach to the Smiths' house with care nevertheless. The last thing he wanted to do was to make the mistake his mentor constable had made and drive the Smith brothers into using their back way in by stationing himself to spy on them from anywhere too obvious.

But he did have to venture as near as the actual street off which their alley led. He walked along it quickly, but not too quickly, all the while making a discreet but thorough inspection of everything in sight.

By daylight the street looked less ominous than it had seemed on the night he had tracked the hulking Pete to his lair. Instead of being sombrely dark, it was merely in the last stages of shabbiness. If not dirty by Bombay standards, it was certainly noticeably less clean than the other London streets Ghote had seen. It had an air everywhere of being ready for the scrap-heap.

A discarded toy pram lay on its side in one of the gutters. Bits of paper were being blown here and there by the wind, so strong this afternoon that it seemed to have swept the whole sky clear and left a bright sun to show up the patches of missing slates on the house roofs and the occasional square of cardboard replacing a broken window-pane.

The little shop where the constable had attempted to hide the night before had a piece of paper in its door, Ghote noticed, bearing the scrawled words 'Must close at end of month. No reasonable offer refused.' It seemed to be selling second-hand clothes and old shoes.

At the far end of the street there was a small block of terraced houses which had already been vacated. Ghote thought of the new tall tower which might rise on their ruins and of the bright promise of the Patsys and Renees who would live in it. A demolition contractor's colourful signboard hung on the rusted railing which protected their deep, sunless little areas. Their windows, long ago smashed and replaced by sheets of silver-grey corrugated iron, looked like the sightless eyes of a row of aged crones sitting waiting for death.

But the sight sent a quick flicker of joy springing up in Ghote's mind. The houses might very well be exactly what he needed.

He hurried along to them and turned to look back. Yes, he had a clear view of the entrance archway of the Smiths' alley. He darted a glance up and down the length of the street. A bunch of children had appeared at the other end, chasing about and shouting. But otherwise there was no one to be seen.

He caught hold of the top of the rusty railings of the nearest house, swung himself up and dropped over into the rubbish-strewn area below. He selected an old wooden crate, carefully placed it in position and got up on it.

As he had hoped, the top of his head came just above the level of the pavement. He was nicely inconspicuous low down like this, and he had a good unobstructed view of the alley archway about thirty yards away.

He settled down to keep it under observation.

Before setting out he had decided, influenced a little by the cheerful sunniness of the day, not to take his overcoat. If he needed to stand somewhere without attracting attention, he had reasoned, its vivid check might be a disadvantage. Now he began to regret the decision. The cement wall in front of him was green with damp and struck chill to the touch whenever he put his hand on it, and stray tail-ends of the boisterous wind seemed to find their way with unpleasant frequency into his little sunken observation post.

But he shrugged his shoulders resignedly. A bit of

discomfort would be a small price to pay for making any reasonable advance with his investigation.

Time passed. An occasional small cloud, cotton-wool white round the edges, soft grey at the centre, momentarily obscured the sun from time to time and was then whisked on its way by the sharp wind.

Ghote stood on his crate looking steadily in the direction of the alley. Waiting.

And then suddenly, from somewhere just beside and behind him, there came an ear-splitting yell. He was so startled he jumped like a triggered-off spring.

"Ere. Look. Look at this.'

He stole a glance round out of the corner of his eye. Clinging to the railings of the steps of the empty house next door was a small girl, perhaps about seven or eight years old. She was wearing a dirty pair of green trousers, a pink frilly blouse heavily smeared with grime and a ragged royal-blue cardigan. Her cheeks were a bright red and she had two little glinting brown button-eyes.

At the sound of her yell, three other children immediately appeared on the steps and stared down at Ghote. They were all a year or so younger than the girl, two boys in pullovers and torn short trousers and a smaller girl with a lemon-yellow coat, buttonless and mud-splashed, clutched tightly round her.

Ghote turned his eyes to the front again.

'It's a nig-nog,' he heard one of the gang say. 'I can see 'is face. It's a nig-nog.'

There was a lot of giggling.

'What's 'e doing down there?' one of the boys said.

'It's a nig-nog.'

'No, but what's 'e doing? What's 'e doing standing down there like that?'

'I know,' said the other boy, his voice phenomenally hoarse. 'I know. 'E ain't real. 'E ain't really real at all.'

'What, you mean 'e's a statue or somethink?'

'Yeah. 'E's a bleeding statue.'

156

'Go on. 'E ain't.'

'I bet 'e is.'

'Bet 'e ain't.'

Standing with his back to them, still looking over at the empty archway, Ghote thought the argument was going to go on all afternoon. But the older girl was plainly one of nature's leaders. Before more than half a dozen further exchanges of recrimination had passed she produced a simple solution to their dilemna.

''Ere, Melv,' she yelled. 'Chuck this at 'im. That'll prove it.'

There were a few incoherent expressions of encouragement and advice. Ghote wondered if he ought to turn round, but he felt that any move he made would only encourage further speculation.

Then something struck him sharply just above the left ear. He looked down as a glinting-edged fragment of bottle-glass bounced off the top of the crate at his feet.

'There. Told you so. 'E's real all right.'

The argument had been settled. Perhaps they would drift away now.

But other questions remained.

'What's 'e doing there though?'

''E's a nig-nog. I keep telling yer. 'E's a nig-nog.'

Ghote suddenly flung himself round.

'Go away,' he said. 'Go away. Now. At once. Be off.'

The button-eyed girl looked down at him in a passion of delight.

'Shan't,' she yelled. 'Shan't. Dirty old nig nog.'

Apparently the yell was the only form of expression she allowed herself. Ghote thought of her voice ringing up and down the comparatively deserted street. Nothing could be better calculated to attract the maximum of attention.

'Listen,' he said rapidly, 'will you go if I give you sixpence?'

The button-eyed girl almost thrust her red-cheeked

157

face through the railings in her pleasure at having provoked such a reaction.

'Sixpence each?' she asked.

That had not been Ghote's intention. And he suspected that she well knew it.

'Yes,' he said. 'Sixpence each.'

'And one for Melv's brother what's got the cough?'

'And one for him.'

For a moment the girl calculated.

'Make it a bob for me, and we're on,' she said.

Ghote delved into his pocket. He could find only two two-shilling pieces. He pulled them out and held them up to the girl.

'You can have this,' he said.

He had no doubt that whatever division of the spoils she decided on, she would have no trouble in enforcing her will.

A grubby little hand scraped the two coins from his palm.

'Coo, thanks, mister.'

And, a bargain being a bargain, in a moment the whole gang had vanished.

Ghote looked up at the sky. It was still a deep, gay blue with clouds whisking across it under the impetus of the chill wind. He looked over at the archway. Still not the least sign of life.

The minutes crawled by.

A bigger cloud than usual moved over the sun. In the damp area it seemed even colder. Ghote shivered.

And then it began to rain. The cloud that was blotting out the sun was greyer than the ones that had preceded it and from it long spearing drops of cold rain fell in a rapid crescendo. Ghote's regret for his big green-and-yellow checked overcoat touched poignancy.

In a moment it became even keener. Before his astonished eyes the pavement in front of him turned in a matter of moments into a sheet of the purest white. His first thought was that this was snow, and he felt, in spite of the way he was getting colder and colder at every instant, a curious thrill of delight. So this was snow, the snow he had read about, wondered about, and even been made to learn a poem at school about, 'On Linden when the sun was low, All bloodless lay the untrodden snow.'

But then the stinging force with which he was being lashed at from above made him realise that this was not in fact snow at all. It was only hail. Every bit as cold, more penetrating to the unprotected clothes, not unknown even in Bombay, and not at all reminiscent of the merry old England of long ago.

He bowed his head and suffered the battering.

When it finished, after what seemed hours but was in fact less than ten minutes, his jacket was wet right through to the skin of his shoulders and the slow, cold dampness was spreading inexorably downwards. The blood seemed to have stopped running in his veins entirely. His fingers were numb to the knuckles and his feet were like two lumps of frozen lead.

He did not think he could be more miserable. And on the far side of the road the archway was obstinately blank and empty. He gritted his chattering teeth and vowed that, come what might, he was not going to budge from his post. It would be getting dark before long, but he was not going to give up. He would wait through the evening, until midnight, until midnight had struck to the last stroke. And only then would he allow himself to go.

Along the street in front of him a mother, pushing a battered pram piled high with groceries from the Portobello Road and trailing a howling child, came hurrying by. But she would be on her way home. A stoked-up fire would greet her.

And then, just as the last of the day was disappearing from the now once more blue sky, there was a sudden movement in the blank archway. Ghote stirred, stamped his feet a little and peered hard across the roadway.

From out of the dark rectangle of the arch there came a dog, Pete's dog, the low-bellied black cur. Ghote watched it with mounting excitement. Did this mean that Pete himself was on his way out? He might even be coming with Jack and Billy, off to spend a Saturday evening on the tiles.

The dog nosed its way on to the pavement and stood sniffing the hail-cleaned air. Then it trotted across the road almost straight towards him.

Ghote hardly paid it any attention now. His eyes were riveted on the archway. Was Pete going to follow?

But the archway remained tantalisingly empty, and the little low-bellied black dog came nosing its way along the railings. He gave it a quick glance. The animal, attracted by the sudden movement at its own level, moved towards him briskly. It came right up to him. Ghote looked at it. It looked back at him. He hoped nothing would make the creature decide that he was something suspicious. If it took it into its head to put back its legs and start off barking, Pete might well come lumbering across to see what was the matter. And, down in the pit of the neglected area, there would be no chance of escape.

But the dog seemed content with what it had seen. It turned indifferently away as if to move off. Then it came to an indecisive halt. It sat down and scratched itself behind the ear. Then it got up and stretched. And then it lifted its leg against the rusty railings.

Ghote felt a strong-smelling warm shower gently pattering down on top of him. He shut his eyes.

Quite soon it stopped. Ghote opened his eyes. He was seized with a sudden panic that during his brief moment of humiliation the three brothers might have for some inexplicable reason made a concerted dash out of the archway. But the dark street was silent and empty. The black dog was the only living thing in sight, wandering unconcernedly towards its home.

Another hour wore by. Two or three cars swished past

in either direction. At the end of the street there was the sound of a sudden quarrel between two loud-mouthed women. But it ended as quickly as it had begun.

Every now and again Ghote allowed himself the luxury of shifting his position and of holding up his wrist so as to see his watch in the light of the nearest street-lamp. He found that on average he went for six minutes between each such moment of respite.

And then, just as he had imagined it would during all the long spell of waiting, it happened. Into the black oblong of the archway there came an abrupt stirring of noise and movement and the three Smith brothers walked nonchalantly out, turned in the direction of the Porto-bello Road and, chatting loudly together, strolled happily away.

Ghote gave them only five minutes.

He reckoned that the sooner he began trying to per-suade their mother to talk the better. Her sons would hardly turn round and come back straight away but they might well content themselves with a single drink at the Duke of Wellington and then come home. And, besides, the quicker he got to Mrs Smith the quicker he would feel the warmth of those paraffin stoves he had heard her talking about.

Stiff with cold, he hobbled across the road, in at the archway, still thick with milk-bottles although they had all been set upright once more, and across to the painfully familiar broken-edged steps of the Smith house.

He hammered hard on the paintless door.

Fourteen

For a long time Ghote's tattoo on the paintless door remained unanswered. Could old Ma Smith have been out of the house the whole time he had been watching it?

But at last there came a dragging, swishing sound from inside. He imagined Mrs Smith in her soft slippers slowly making her way towards him. And a moment later the door was opened and there she was, looking so exactly as he had seen her before that he wondered if she ever removed the huge closely-flowered apron, the sagging purple cardigan and the battered but bright red slippers with the one missing pom-pom.

She glanced up at him and vaguely pushed aside the trailing lock of dark grey hair from in front of her broad, snub-nosed face.

'It's a bloody black,' she said in a tone of mild wonder. 'You're not the one that came round the other night, are you?'

'Yes,' Ghote admitted. 'I was here.'

He attempted a friendly smile before making his request.

'Could we perhaps go inside?' he asked. 'I have a matter I would like to discuss with you.'

Mrs Smith blinked at him slowly.

'Look, mate,' she said, without rancour, 'just hop it, won't you?'

She put her hand to the door to close it. But she was by no means a quick mover, and Ghote had plenty of time quietly to lean his shoulder against the jamb.

'Please,' he said, 'it will only take five minutes, and it is very important to me. It is about a girl who is missing. My niece.'

He decided that a certain simplification of his relation-

162

ship with the Peacock was justified.

'I can't help that,' Ma Smith replied, not uncheerfully. 'I mean, if it's one black the fewer, well, it's good riddance really, isn't it?'

She looked at Ghote with some curiosity, as if to see what form his agreement would take.

'But she is missing, missing,' he pleaded. 'Please imagine. What would you feel if one of your children suddenly disappeared?'

Mrs Smith broke into a deep chuckle.

'What, one of my boys disappear?' she said. 'I'd like to see it, really I would. Those boys couldn't no more disappear than what Nelson's Column could.'

The sheer pride in her voice seemed to spread out in waves into the night air.

Ghote saw at once that this was what he had to latch on to.

'Well, no,' he agreed heartily, 'I can see that they are hardly the sort to disappear. Three such fine, big men as they are.'

'You won't find bigger,' Mrs Smith said comfortably. 'And you won't find better.'

Ghote felt a little shock of surprise. Surely Mrs Smith must have some idea of her sons' mode of life. They plainly were not the sort to go out every day to steady jobs, and yet they must always have enough money for drinking and going dancing. Had she really contrived not to know they were criminals?

'Yes,' he agreed, rather hesitantly, 'they seem to be really good men.'

'Good as they come,' Mrs Smith said. 'Why, you ought to see the way they furnished this place for me in the past few years since my old man passed on. Come in. Look.'

And, smiling to himself inwardly, Ghote followed her into the house, down the dark narrow passage where Billy had so nearly beaten him up, and in through the first door they came to.

He found himself in a kitchen-cum-living-room, and in

such overwhelming warmth that it was like stepping back into somewhere in steamy, humid Bombay again. He thawed in seconds.

On two of the walls, he saw, there were smart, double-burner paraffin stoves, the air above them shimmering with heat, and in the fireplace there stood a big three-bar electric fire, each bar pulsatingly aglow.

Ma Smith waddled across to a low, cushion-filled arm-chair beside the fire and sank gratefully down. She saw Ghote looking round.

'Yeh,' she said, 'it's a lovely room, ain't it? And every blessed thing in it nicked by one of my boys or another. Look at that telly. Did you ever see a telly like that?'

Ghote looked across at the television set standing on the shelf of a big old dresser among an incredible clutter of other objects – cornflake packets, plates and dishes, half-empty bottles, dirty tea-cups, a loudly ticking alarm-clock. The set certainly looked magnificent. It had a huge screen, a gleaming polished wood cabinet and a glinting array of smart black-and-gold knobs.

Then his eyes widened. Standing on top of this luxurious monster was the most enormous glossy calendar he had ever set eyes on, a splendid plastic affair showing the whole year at a glance and rainbow-coloured with various pictures of landmarks of London – Trafalgar Square, Piccadilly Circus, the Houses of Parliament, Westminster Abbey and, of course, the Tower that he had yet to get to see. But more magnetically attractive to him than even this was a single dark-pencilled ring round one solitary date, a day late in October. He strained towards it but he could not for certain make out which.

'Yeh, my Billy noticed the set in a shop-window,' Ma Smith continued happily. 'He saw it was better than the one what we had. And, do you know, he did the place that very night.'

Ghote felt at a loss for a reply. He did not want to condone burglary: but he was more than anxious to keep

164

on the right side of Mrs Smith.

'It certainly looks a fine set,' he compromised at last.

'Yeh, well, you wouldn't know,' Mrs Smith said cheerfully. 'Not coming from where you come from, being savages and that.'

In view of the fact that at any moment Mrs Smith's light-fingered, heavy-fisted sons might choose to come back home, Ghote thought he would not mention India's achievements in the field of technology. Mrs Smith would take a long time to convince.

A way of leading the conversation in the direction of the ringed date on the big calendar, still tantalisingly too far away to be certain of, occurred to him.

'With such sons as you have,' he said, 'do you ever worry that they will get married and leave you?'

'Married?' Mrs Smith laughed richly. 'What would they want to get married for? They can get all the girls they want without marrying.'

'Ah yes, I suppose so. It would be a very strong-minded girl indeed who would be able to resist them.'

'That's right. Been like that since they were thirteen or fourteen, they have. Ah, we've had some good laughs when they've told me some of the things they've done. Some good giggles we've had over it all.'

'I expect so,' said Ghote coldly.

Then, recollecting himself, he made a hasty addition.

'You are lucky to have such entertaining children.'

'And kind,' Ma Smith added, looking fondly at the television set.

'Yes,' said Ghote. 'I suppose they tell you almost everything that they do?'

'Well, I like a good gossip,' Mrs Smith conceded.

'Yes, yes.'

Ghote produced something like a jovial laugh.

'So you will know all about my niece?' he said. 'Billy will have told you everything?'

Ma Smith looked at him from the sprawling comfort of

her chair.

'Was that the one you were talking about just now?' she asked.

'Yes, that is the one,' Ghote said noncommittally.

'The one what's gone missing?'

'Yes, she is missing.'

He tried to take out of his voice any shade of condemnation for anything that Billy might have done.

'I don't know about her,' Mrs Smith said placidly.

The suspicions redoubled in Ghote's mind.

'Then there are things your sons do not tell you?' he said with a touch of sharpness.

A look of mild bewilderment appeared on Mrs Smith's snub-nosed face.

'Well, I did think they told me most things,' she said. 'Unless they forgot.'

She sat looking at the blank screen of the huge television set, as if it was just possible an explanation of the puzzling circumstances might be flashed on to it in picture form. Ghote edged a foot nearer to the set, and to the great glossy calendar on top of it.

He strained to see.

And, yes, it was the date. It was October the twenty-first that had been ringed so heavily round.

He felt a single swift leap of excitement.

''Ere,' said Ma Smith suddenly, 'that's not the girl they call the Peacock, is it? Funny name for a girl I always thought, the Peacock.'

'Yes, yes,' said Ghote eagerly. 'That is her.'

'Yeh, my Billy did mention her once or twice, now I come to think of it. Quite fancied her, he did. I dare say he'll make out all right in a day or two.'

She frowned.

'Or did you say she's gone off?' she added.

'But do you not know what happened on the night of October the twenty-first?' Ghote burst out.

For once Ma Smith moved with some speed. She turned

166

round sharply in her wide-spreading chair and looked at him.

'The night of the twenty-first,' she said. 'Of course I know what happened then.'

A tiny, subdued drum-beat of pleasure began to pulse out in Ghote's mind. Was he at last getting to the very heart of it? He must be.

'Please tell me,' he said. 'Please.'

'Well, I can't see as how you've got all that right to know.'

'Please, Mrs Smith, I want very much just to hear.'

It was a weak plea. But apparently it was enough.

'Well, all right, if you're so keen.'

Mrs Smith shrugged and settled herself comfortably in the big chair again.

'It was more what happened all day on the twenty-first than the night,' she said. 'Though of course it was the night that mattered.'

'Yes?' said Ghote, almost holding his breath.

'Yeh. And the next morning with that old judge. Though that turned out all right in the end.'

'That old judge?'

'Yeh. You know. What they called a Judge in Chambers.'

'I am afraid I do not understand.'

Mrs Smith gave another of her deep chuckles.

'Well, you're no better off than what I am then,' she said. ''Cos I'm blessed if I understand too much about it meself.'

'But I do not understand what you are talking about at all.'

Mrs Smith frowned.

'Well, I'm talking about when the coppers thought they'd got my boys, of course,' she said.

'And when was that?'

Again a mild frown appeared on Ma Smith's broad forehead.

'Well, it was the twenty-first of October. I thought that was what we were talking about.'

'And what exactly happened then?' Ghote asked, still groping in a sea of blackness.

'Like I told you. The boys had been doing a job, and the coppers nearly caught 'em at it. Took 'em in, they did. And brought 'em up before the beak next day. Well, that would've been all right, only the old fool wouldn't let 'em have no bail.'

'No bail?'

'No. So they was kept in the cells. Well, of course the boys weren't having that. Naturally.'

'Naturally,' agreed Ghote.

'So they got this lawyer they have again. The one what gets 'em off when they've been caught up with.'

'I see.'

'And in the end he fixed it up for 'em all right. It was all in the papers. He had to go to this Judge in Chambers. But he couldn't get hold of him till next morning. And why they was in Chambers I couldn't say. Always thought a chamber was something quite different, if you take my meaning.'

Mrs Smith laughed richly and wheezily.

'So let me get it clear,' Ghote said, with a cold gulp. 'They spent the night of October the twenty-first in a police-station waiting till the Judge in Chambers gave them bail?'

He had to get it absolutely straight: it meant the collapse of his whole patient investigation. He had to have it confirmed beyond possibility of error.

'Yeh, yeh. That's right,' Mrs Smith said. 'That's why the date's ringed round on the calendar there. The only night they ever spent in the cells, my boys.'

She fell to looking broodingly at the three fiercely burning bars of the electric fire at her feet.

Ghote turned round and very quietly walked out.

Once again Ghote took every precaution to avoid an encounter with Mrs Datta or her husband on his return to the Tagore House. He had gone on foot all the way back from the Smiths' trying to get the situation into perspective, but even when he reached the restaurant, with the aromatic odour of its curries wafting out into the street all round and the rich glow of light from its discreetly curtained windows, he still had by no means got things straight. So he went quietly round to the entrance at the back and crept up the stairs like a ghost.

Sitting on the edge of his bed, the bed that had once been the Peacock's, he made one final effort to order his thoughts.

Look at it how he might, he could not get round what Ma Smith had told him. All three of the brothers had been in police-station cells from before the time the Peacock had disappeared until well afterwards. No wonder the constable had said they were already in trouble enough. But however much trouble they were in, it could have absolutely nothing to do with the Peacock vanishing when she had.

He would have to get hold of a newspaper of the day after the brothers had got their bail from the Judge in Chambers. He could hardly simply take Ma Smith's word for it. But, once he had that confirmation, the trail he had followed with so much difficulty would have come to an abrupt end. What next?

There was, of course, Robin. He had sold the Peacock drugs. He would have to be seen again. And there was Johnny Bull. There were still circumstances connected with him which were to a certain degree unsatisfactory.

But neither line promised one quarter as well as the case against the Smith brothers had done. With a heavy heart, Ghote undressed and got into bed.

On Sunday morning he straight away encountered another setback. Although Cousin Vidur put all his waiters to work looking for an old newspaper of October the twenty-third, there was not one to be found.

So it was in a mood of checked fury mingled with black depression that, shortly before eleven o'clock, he set out to visit the Robin's Nest once again.

Nor did the sight of the little café itself, with its hectically red-breasted robin so badly painted on the door, do anything to lift his gloom. He almost turned away without so much as going in. But the remnants of pride he felt in doing a job till it was done to the last detail pushed him on and he swung the door back and entered.

He was at once greeted by a blast of unexpected sound. He had not bothered to look inside before going in and it had not occurred to him that at this hour of the morning there would be any customers. But there were. A group of half a dozen teenage girls, all long coloured stockings, mini-skirts and quilted anoraks, clustered round the ancient, patchily spruced-up juke box which for their benefit was going full blast. The robin in the bright blue cage on the top was hopping up and down and round about in a perfect frenzy of delight.

In a moment Ghote recognised the tune. It was the same one as he had heard here before, Johnny Bull singing 'It's Love, Only Love.'

Beyond the girls he saw Robin, busy with his back to the door cutting sandwiches. It did not look as if the girls were making much demand on his services.

Ghote marched up to the counter and tapped on it sharply.

Robin turned. And at the sight of Ghote his round ruddy face with its little beak of a nose went almost comically blank with dismay. He stared and stared as if, try as he might, he could not believe the evidence of his senses.

At last he spoke, trying to keep his voice down under the pounding sound of the juke box.

'You,' he said. 'You. I never expected to see you round here. And you look all right too.'

He stopped and stared again, as if to make sure this was indeed the man he had set the Smith brothers on to.

'Yes,' said Ghote, with a strong touch of grimness, 'I am here, and lucky that is for you. If what you had expected had happened to me, I would have seen that you paid for it.'

Robin opened his round little mouth once or twice. But there was nothing he could say, and he knew it.

'Now then,' said Ghote, not bothering to keep his voice low, 'there is also more to it. There is the matter of your lying.'

'Lying?'

Robin hurriedly stifled the high pitch of his retort.

'I never told a lie in me life,' he whispered passionately.

'Stop that straight away.'

'Well,' Robin conceded with a gulp, 'I may tell a lie or two every now and again. But only when strictly necessary, you know. Only when strictly necessary.'

'So why was it necessary to lie to me about the date Billy Smith left here with the Peacock?' Ghote asked sharply.

'The date when Billy left with the girl?' Robin whispered strenuously. 'I never told you a word of a lie over that. I swear I didn't.'

'You told me it was on the night of October the twenty-first, Trafalgar Day.'

Robin's round, ruddy face was crossed by an expression of hurt.

'Well, how could I be expected to know when Trafalgar Day was?' he said in the same earnest whisper. 'It's all the same to me, I tell you, Trafalgar Day, St George's Day, Empire Day. What they want to have 'em all for, I don't know.'

'But you said that it was on October the twenty-first.'

'Did I? Did I? Well, if I said that, it must have been, mustn't it?'

'But Billy Smith was in a police-station cell on the night of October the twenty-first.'

Robin's podgy little hand flew to his mouth as if he had inadvertently made a rude noise.

'Was that the day?' he squeaked. 'Well, fancy that. Then he couldn't have been in here, could he?'

'No,' said Ghote, 'he could not. So why did you say he was?'

Robin looked quickly from side to side. From the juke box under the wildly hopping pet bird the voice of Johnny Bull repeating, endlessly it seemed, the words 'It's love, only love' bawled deafeningly on. The girls bunched squeezingly round it.

'I'm afraid I made a mistake, that's all,' Robin said.

He put his beaky little nose in the air and looked at Ghote challengingly.

'You made a mistake?' Ghote snapped. 'A very likely story. You wanted to cover your tracks at all costs, I think.'

'Tracks? What tracks?'

'You wanted to conceal from me that you had a great deal more to do with the Peacock than you were willing to have known. That is why you rang up the Smith brothers while I was there and tried to get them to shut me up. You could not do it yourself.'

Robin clutched at the edge of his well-polished counter with both hands.

'I'm sure I have no idea what you could be meaning,' he said.

'You know just exactly what I am meaning.'

'No. No, I swear I don't.'

He darted a glance at the still absorbed bunch of girls.

'Then I will tell you,' Ghote said. 'I am meaning that you sold that poor girl drugs and –'

'Ssssh,' said Robin frantically.

He looked at the girls. They had obviously heard nothing.

'I already told you about that,' he whispered. 'And anyway it was more like she sold them to herself. She must have 'em: needed them to get back her boy-friend, if you

172

please. Pester. Pester. Pester. I simply couldn't get rid of her.'

Ghote thrust himself half-way across the counter.

'I suggest that is just what you did do,' he said. 'In the end you got rid of her.'

A look of purest indignation came on to Robin's round face.

'Me?' he said.

The word came out as a shrill, irritated squeak. But he no longer attempted to keep his voice down.

'Me? You're saying I did away with that poor kid?'

He shook his head incredulously from side to side.

'You're saying I got rid of her,' he repeated. 'With the customers never out of the place from seven in the morning till two at night? Do you think I can commit a murder between serving cups of coffee? You must be joking. You really must be joking.'

Rather than go back to the Tagore House and face the possibility of becoming involved in explaining the present state of his investigation, Ghote decided to go straight from the Robin's Nest to Johnny Bull's flat at the Carlton Tower. It was not a propect that filled him with pleasure. But Johnny was now his last slender hope of finding out what had happened to the Peacock. Her relations with him were the last part of her life that held anything of mystery, and he had to discover something in them which would account for her disappearance. He had to.

So, without allowing himself even a moment's delay, he consulted his by now rather battered London guide and made his way directly from the Portobello Road to Sloane Street. And, again forbidding himself even five minutes to walk up and down the broad pavement outside the huge, glossy hotel on the excuse of needing to order his thoughts, he went round to the entrance to the private suites and almost flung himself into the black-and-gold, silent and rapid lift.

At Johnny Bull's floor, he marched straight out of the

lift and across to the door of Johnny's flat. He put his thumb firmly on the stainless steel bellpush.

There was no answer.

He rang again. He rang once more. He rang at intervals of thirty seconds for five whole minutes. But no one came to the door.

He went down by the lift and made a cautious inquiry from the voluminously coated, much medalled commissionaire. Yes, Mr Bull had gone out early. He had taken his Jaguar. He, and the lady, often spent Sunday in the country. He usually got back very late.

Ghote went, tail between his legs, home to the Tagore House. And as soon as he had let himself in at the back door he encountered Mrs Datta. She was standing at the top of the stairs and seemed very glad to see him.

'Ah, Cousin,' she said. 'I have been waiting for you. Come up. Come up.'

Ghote hung his heavy coat on the little row of hooks, stroked the rough surface of its cloth once for reassurance and mounted the stairs.

Cousin Vidur was also in the sitting-room. He was standing, as usual, in front of the gasfire, which was popping away as merrily as ever. Mrs Datta had, it seemed, finished the piece of deep purple knitting and had begun on a piece of strident green, which she had already picked up before Ghote entered. It was growing fast under her restless fingers.

But her task did not stop her immediately fixing Ghote with a keen look.

'It is time you told us what you are finding out about my Peacock,' she said.

Ghote smiled a little.

'I have had a great deal to do,' he answered. 'There has been not only my investigation, but there is the conference. There is a lot of hard work in that.'

'And your investigation?' Mrs Datta said. 'Where has that led you to?'

174

Ghote clasped his hands together in front of him and rubbed the knuckles of the right hand in the palm of the left.

'I am making a certain amount of progress,' he advanced guardedly.

'Yes, yes.'

'Yes, I think I can say that. It is as much a question of eliminating certain lines of inquiry as anything. But that is a very necessary part of any investigation.'

He shot Cousin Vidur, over by the bottle-lined mantelpiece, a quick look.

'Certainly it must be necessary to find out what has not happened,' Vidur agreed solemnly.

For the first time Ghote felt sympathetic towards him. He had a good deal of common sense after all.

Mrs Datta's voice from low down on her couch broke sharply in.

'You went to the house of these criminals called Smith?' she asked.

'Yes, yes. That was a line that had to be pursued. Definitely.'

'And you have found where they are keeping my Peacock?'

'They are not keeping her.'

Mrs Datta's head shot up from her bottle-green knitting.

'Then why did you go to their house?'

Ghote sighed. Loudly and clearly.

'That was one of the matters it was necessary to eliminate,' he said. 'They had behaved in a most suspicious way, and had in fact offered me personal violence. It was necessary to conduct a most rigorous investigation.'

He looked sternly down at Mrs Datta.

She looked back at him, her spectacles glinting.

'But they were not hiding my Peacock?'

Ghote felt a spasm of fury. He had told the woman that he had run into considerable danger in his hunt for her niece, and was this all the thanks he was to get?

'No,' he said sharply. 'They are not hiding your Peacock. I had to risk entering their house in their absence to discover that.'

Mrs Datta shrugged her bony shoulders under her sari.

'To discover that someone is not where you think they are is not very helpful,' she said. 'Where is she truly? That is the point, you know.'

A jet of pure rage soared through Ghote's head.

'Perhaps it is not the point,' he said. 'Perhaps the point is: who has killed her?'

'That girl could have killed my Peacock,' Mrs Datta unexpectedly replied. 'They could have killed her together.'

'Who could have killed her?'

'Johnny Bull and that girl.'

Ghote blinked.

'You mean the girl Sandra?'

'If that is her name.'

'But why should she have killed her? Why are we talking about her? I do not understand.'

An ugly suspicion that he did understand perfectly well could not altogether be suppressed.

'You do not understand,' Mrs Datta replied, unperturbed by the fact that Ghote was beginning to shout, 'because you are all the time looking for who did not take away my Peacock. You must start to look for who did take her.'

Ghote felt tears of despair coming into his eyes.

'It is the same thing,' he said, forcing himself to speak calmly. 'Finding out who did not do a thing is the other half of finding out who did do it.'

'It is Johnny who did it,' Mrs Datta replied. 'Johnny and Sandra.'

She gave her full attention to her knitting again. Ghote, in desperation, turned to Cousin Vidur for support.

Vidur, legs plumply apart in front of the little orange fire, looked grave.

'Yes,' he said, 'from what you have told that girl is certainly the worst type of Westerner. To hang around a man like that disgusting Johnny Bull with decadent music always on his lips. It is nothing short of scandalous. Yes, scandalous.'

He gave an emphatic nod to indicate that his judgment was concluded and relapsed into silence.

Ghote could not refrain from shooting him a glance of quick anger. But he appeared not to notice it. For an instant Ghote was tempted to shout out to his face that he knew him to be nothing but a drug-sodden old *afim-wallah*. But he found he had not got the heart somehow.

Vidur deflated would be a sight so pathetic that it was worth enduring hours of Vidur inflated to avoid.

He looked from husband to wife, from wife to husband Neither appeared to have any further comments to make. The nasty thought that what Mrs Datta had said about Johnny and Sandra, however unlikely, was a technical possibility, and one that he had left out of account, could no longer be fought down.

'Well,' he said, his voice sounding even to his own ears over-loud and strained, 'to-morrow morning, in any case, I am going to see Johnny Bull and Sandra. First thing.'

But before the time came to see Johnny Bull again a more pressing anxiety had obtruded itself. In the morning post on Monday there was a short note from Superintendent Smart. It told him that owing to a slight change of circumstances he was to deliver Superintendent Ketkar's paper to the Drugs Conference next day, Tuesday. 'We all look forward to it with the keenest interest, as well as to hearing your own views,' the letter concluded.

If there had been one thing to be grateful for in all the unpleasantness of his search for the Peacock, it had been that he had had no time to think about this particular ordeal. But now the thought could no longer be pushed away.

To suit the convenience of the Continental delegates to

177

the conference there was to be no meeting on Monday morning. Ghote had confidently earmarked the time for his second interview with Johnny Bull. But he knew now that he must first confront the brooding spirit of Superintendent Ketkar. Nevertheless he promised himself he would still get to the Carlton Tower before Johnny Bull took it into his head to go for another day in the country, especially as the weather was still bright, if not warm.

So, up in the sanctuary of the Peacock's room at the top of the house, he extracted the superintendent's slim, stiffly bound typescript from its resting place in his case.

But the actual sight of it brought on an unwillingness even to look at its contents which was almost physical. Eventually he made the effort and turned to the first page. The words stared back at him as if they had been written in some unknown language.

They continued to do so until he decided that, before embarking on a full-scale rehearsal, he ought just to flip through the whole paper to familiarise himself again with the main outlines of its argument.

And having managed in this way to get to the end, if not exactly to absorb every turn of the superintendent's train of thought, he hastily pushed the stiff folder back in his case and hurried off to the Carlton Tower with feelings almost of pleasure.

Pausing only to arrange at the newspaper shop a couple of doors away from the restaurant to collect the following day copies of all the papers in which the story of the Smith brothers and the Judge in Chambers was likely to have appeared, he made his way rapidly to the bus-stop and stood waiting for a Number 137 bus.

So it was still only a few minutes after ten o'clock when he rang once more at the richly discreet, stainless steel bellpush on Johnny Bull's front door. And this time there was no long period of waiting.

The door in fact opened so promptly that his carefully prepared opening sentence totally deserted him and he stood blinking and silent.

It was Sandra who had been so quick to open the door. Dressed in a glowing purple trouser-suit, which made her pale, podgy face look even paler and more featureless than Ghote had remembered it, she looked up at him now with an expression of rapidly growing petulance.

'You,' she said. 'What the hell are you doing here? I thought it was Freddy.'

'Who is Freddy?' Ghote asked.

Evidently his question, which he would have been the first to admit was not strictly relevant to the business he had come on, served only to redouble the girl's minute rage.

'Freddy's Johnny's publicist, of course,' she snapped. 'He's due any minute to take him to the studios.'

'Oh, dear,' Ghote said. 'I had hoped to have a few words with Mr Bull. But perhaps there will be time still. I would not keep him very long.'

A look of shocked amazement contrived to imprint itself on Sandra's pale featureless face.

'No, you will not keep him,' she said. 'And, no, you will not see him. Not now, or ever.'

She began to swing the door closed.

Ghote, ready for this, slid his foot forward. And, just at the moment when the sharp edge of the door banged hard on to the inside of his instep, there came a roar of sound from the flat.

'Where is it? What the bloody hell have you done with it?'

It was Johnny Bull himself. Sandra whipped round as if somebody behind her had shouted 'Stick 'em up.'

'Never mind about it,' she yelled. 'You've got a bloody long day ahead of you, and I mean to see you get to those studios on time.'

Over her shoulder, at the far end of the broad, white-carpeted, record-hung corridor Ghote could just see Johnny. He was wearing nothing but a pair of black-and-white pyjama trousers. The thick fuzz of dark hair on his chest impressed itself on Ghote's mind.

'Studios,' Johnny shouted back at plump little Sandra. 'Bloody studios. Bloody, bloody Regent Studios. I'm not going there to-day.'

'Oh yes you are,' Sandra screamed back, with a violence Ghote would not have thought her capable of.

And then something must have reminded her that she was under observation still, because she swung round again, gave Ghote a look of passionate dislike, and, putting hand to the back of the door, brought it crashing towards him with all the strength of her whole body.

He judged it best to whip his foot out of the way.

In any case, he thought, I know all I need to now.

As he walked over to the black-and-gold lift he heard her yelling a final message to him through the smooth and inscrutable surface of the heavy door.

'And don't come back, because he's not going to see you. Ever.'

Fifteen

Most of the morning still lay ahead of Ghote when he left the Carlton Tower, hugging to himself the knowledge that Johnny Bull was due to spend 'a long day' at the Regent Studios. It should not be difficult to find out where these were, and the day's activities at the Drugs Conference were certain to be over before Johnny's day's work.

He knew that what he ought to do in the time he had to spare was to go back to his little room at the Tagore House, take out Superintendent Ketkar's typescript, open it at Page One and start reading aloud in a clear, ringing voice. But he could not force himself to take the plunge. The distance between what he ought to achieve and what he knew with despondent certainty he could actually manage was simply too great. He had had to address small bodies of men every now and again in the course of his career, and he was aware that, although he did not do it particularly well, he could at least make a reasonable showing. But this business of being Superintendent Ketkar, and in front of a distinguished and critical audience, was altogether different. It was an Everest: he was equipped with only light summer clothing.

Then a comforting thought swam into his head: it was his duty to get Protima her present. The task had been put off too long.

Of course he could have indulged himself, he could have gone on his postponed visit to the Tower. There was just nice time for it. But, no, he would tackle this urgent duty first.

He took out his guide book with the look of someone resolutely shunning delights and facing the sound of gunfire. He looked for the quickest way to Oxford Street.

Emerging from the Tube, he made his way along the broad pavement with its strongly moving crowd of shoppers, buying, buying, buying as they moved. Their crammed, bright and gaily patterned shopping-bags bumped and banged him and their strident yammering voices battered at his ears. 'Well, as I say, they're only kids once, get 'em the best, I say' . . . 'must have some marrons glacés for Auntie May, though what she sees in 'em I don't know' . . . 'can't think what to get our Dad, never seems to want anything' . . . 'Yes, I bought her some nice perfume, paid a bit more than I expected though, but I must get her something to last too.'

He began to feel the need to creep quietly away from it all – the stately matrons with their elaborate hair-styles, the mothers with their petulant children forging their way along to the accompaniment of a perpetual jagged whine of meaningless rebukes, the plump little teenagers with their inevitable mini-skirts.

But these last he suddenly excepted from his bile-black condemnation. His original feelings of dismayed disapproval had, he found, melted away. Perhaps his encounter with Patsy and Renee in their high tower block had given him a new outlook. After all, he reasoned, the girls did breathe an air of half-innocent enjoyment of the gifts nature had given them. They were no doubt much the same as young girls anywhere else, only with more confidence.

Then he found he was reassessing another belief. He noticed beside a fur-coated, stiffly-hatted, triumphant, full-fleshed grandmother – talking incessantly of what she had just purchased and what else she was about to purchase – an oldish man, probably her husband, walking quietly along smoking his pipe. He looked thoroughly comfortable in green pork-pie hat and brown herringbone overcoat and in his eyes there was a mildly amused twinkle.

He reminded Ghote abruptly of Superintendent Smart.

And with the reminder he saw all the strenuous shoppers suddenly in another light. After all, they had got to do something with the money they found they had, and what more simply natural than to spend it? That at least spread it out. The sight of a shop selling goods from India – saris, bangles, brass coffee pots, jewellery, carved elephants – made him realise where in fact some of this disbursed wealth was ending up.

He looked round more cheerfully. And at once he saw what looked like the very place he wanted for his present-getting. It was a shop with its windows crammed full of every sort and kind of chinaware. If he could not find something splendidly English and within his means here, he never would.

He went in. Everywhere there were long tables stacked with gleaming china. He made up his mind to concentrate on tea-services.

But it was not long before he was feeling more than a

little bewildered by the sheer variety even of these. He wondered about what he really wanted and of having to admit how little he could actually afford deterred him. The thought of his first attempt to make his purchase at the big department store had not faded from his mind.

'Can I help you, sir?'

The quiet voice had come from just behind him. He wheeled guiltily round.

The person who had spoken was very different from the proud goddess of the department store. She was motherly-looking, short, very plump and with a faint but distinct moustache on her upper lip.

The contrast between what she looked like and what he had been expecting was so strong that, before he knew what he was doing, he burst out with the thought buried deep in his mind.

'The Royal Worcester you have,' he said, 'is it highly expensive also?'

The assistant smiled.

'Well now, sir,' she said, 'let's not make too many bones about it: it is expensive, yes. But that doesn't mean we haven't heaps of other lovely things which wouldn't cost half as much.'

'Yes,' said Ghote doubtfully. 'I have seen some.'

Again he received a smile.

'I did notice you looking here and there, sir,' the assistant said. 'Something in the line of a tea-service, isn't it?'

'Yes,' Ghote conceded, 'I was looking for a tea-service.'

He declined absolutely to expand on this further.

'Well now,' the assistant said with motherly briskness, 'and who is this tea-service to be for? I always say it makes a lot of difference to know.'

'Yes,' said Ghote.

'Now, is it a present?'

'It is for my wife.'

The assistant gave him a warm smile.

183

'Your wife,' she said. 'But you must tell me a little bit more about her than that, you know. Otherwise I might give you quite the wrong advice.'

'She is in India,' Ghote admitted. 'I want to take her back a gift.'

He found himself strongly reluctant to explain any of the circumstances of his stay in England, let alone to expand on what the present meant to him.

'Oh, yes,' the assistant replied, in a rush of friendliness that altogether swamped his meagre response.

She looked at him warmly.

'I always think it's so nice when a gentleman goes abroad and doesn't fail to come back with something for the lady at home.'

'Yes,' said Ghote.

'And I'm sure, if we look about a bit, we'll hit on just the very thing.'

She gave him another look, carefully considering.

'But,' she added, 'we must be careful not to go spending too much, mustn't we? I know what it is when you go to other countries: everything seems so expensive.'

'But I do not want to take back a present that is cheap,' Ghote said in alarm.

Again he was given a smile of deep understanding.

'Oh no, of course not. We'll find something good, but reasonable. I'm sure you'll be very pleased with it. And the lady need never know just what you paid, need she?'

'But I want it to be something of the best there is in England,' Ghote said.

He had begun to feel suspiciously that things were slipping out of his control, and he spoke with some vehemence.

'Ah, I quite understand,' the assistant replied, unruffled. 'Something that, how shall I put it, something that sums up all our old English delight in beautiful things well made.'

This was exactly what Ghote had had in mind. But,

perversely, he did not feel pleased to hear it said.

He made no reply.

A look of sudden recollection appeared on the assistant's motherly, moustached face.

'Ah,' she said, 'how about this?'

Taking Ghote firmly by the sleeve of his heavy, green-and-yellow coat, she began guiding him through the aisles between the long china-ladden tables. She stopped at last in front of a large display near the shop-windows.

It consisted of nothing but teapots, noble teapots, purest white, gold-edged, sproutingly decorated with clumps of bright painted flowers, a mass of full-bellied, gleaming teapots, redolent each one of the old Britain Ghote loved. Or had certainly loved at the moment when he had first set foot on its soil.

A neat, discreet little folded card in the middle of the display indicated a price that Ghote could certainly afford.

And yet a dark unwillingness to concede that here was the end of his search grew up in him.

'Why is it, please,' he demanded, 'that they are so cheap?'

The assistant smiled.

'More reasonable than cheap,' she corrected him gently.

'But why is it?' Ghote persisted mulishly.

Again there came a warm smile from the dark brown eyes.

'Well, don't mistake my meaning, but they're actually what we call, well, export rejects.'

And, with an inner knowledge that he was not behaving sensibly or gratefully in the least, Ghote let a look of chilling coldness sweep up into his face and spark icily off. He turned on his heel and set off for the door.

'There is nothing I require here,' he said. 'Nothing.'

Even when Ghote, early that afternoon, had settled himself in his place in the handsome conference hall at Wood Street police-station and had his notebook ready open on his knee, he could not calm the inner disturbance his attempt to buy Protima her present had caused him. The ordered dignity of the proceedings in the hall served in fact only to irritate him yet more.

Up on the platform in front of the great sweep of rust-coloured curtaining, Superintendent Smart stood and tapped with his knuckles on the small table in front of him. At once a hush fell. It sent a jet of anger shooting up inside Ghote's head: why could not one delegate, just one, make the mistake of going on talking? Why did every one of them have to be so competent about everything.

'Good afternoon, gentlemen,' Smart of the Yard said, in a quiet voice which was still just loud enough to reach to every part of the hall. 'I trust you all had a pleasant week-end.'

No, thought Ghote with redoubled sourness, I for one did not have a pleasant week-end. I had a most unpleasant week-end. As if it mattered to anybody.

But from the remainder of the delegates there came a subdued acquiescent murmur.

'Before we begin our proceedings again,' Superintendent Smart went on, 'I should just like to say that this is the last occasion we shall meet in these most comfortable surroundings.'

Uncomfortable surroundings, Ghote thought contrarily, looking round at the lofty ceiling, sparkling chandeliers, tall, deeply recessed windows and magnificent swathes of curtaining.

'Owing to the short time we had to make our arrangements,' Superintendent Smart continued, 'we shall have to hold our remaining session elsewhere. But I am happy to be able to tell you that we have secured the auditorium at the Commonwealth Institute in Kensington. Police cadets will hand you on your way out folders giving all the necessary directions.'

He paused and glanced down at the sheet of paper on the table in front of him.

'Now we come to to-day's business,' he resumed. 'And it is perhaps appropriate that, as we are on the verge of moving over to the Commonwealth Institute, our last two speakers should be from the Commonwealth. To-day we have Superintendent Mahommed Jaffer from West Pakistan, and to-morrow we have someone I might call his near neighbour, Inspector Ghote of Bombay, deputising at very short notice for the renowned figure of Superintendent Rakesh Ketkar, whose work all of you will be well acquainted with.'

And at once the delegates broke into an appreciative patter of applause.

Ghote's heart sank. To have this build-up, and then to hear his own halting version of Superintendent Ketkar's forceful and vigorous words. It could not but be disastrous.

But in the next few minutes his heart went even further into his boots. For Superintendent Jaffer, of Karachi – the tall, bearded Pakistani whom he had just failed to talk to when he had first come, diffident and uneasy, into this very room – turned out to be a speaker almost as forceful and humorous as Superintendent Ketkar himself. His trenchant analysis of the drug smuggling situation in his particular part of the world, with a few mischievous asides about matters farther down the west coast of the Indian sub-continent, plainly delighted all the other delegates. There were quick bursts of laughter, appreciative murmurs, a continuing run of deep chuckles and everywhere the rapid scribbling in notepads and on the backs of envelopes which denoted real success.

Scribbling of notes everywhere, except at one place. It was only as, with a final triumphant sally Superintendent Jaffer brought his study to a conclusion, that Ghote realised that so acute had been his mortification, with this paper in particular and everything that had happened to him since he first set foot in England in general, that he had completely and utterly failed to take a single word down. Total misery descended.

Ghote got away from Wood Street police-station as soon as he could, but he found he had little heart for going to get hold of Johnny Bull at the Regent Studios. Before the conference session had begun he had looked them up in a telephone directory. He had found the entry without difficulty: the Regent Recording Studios, a street name and a number. And it had been easy enough to locate the street, in the middle of Marylebone, in his guide book.

More because doing anything else seemed utterly distasteful than out of any positive willingness, he followed out the route he had marked down. It brought him at just after five o'clock to a small blank iron door set deep into a long featureless brick wall in a quiet back street. Beside the door, embedded into the concrete surround, was a small notice in engraved brown plastic saying 'Regent Recording Studios.' There was no bell.

When he put his hand to the iron door itself it began to swing open at his touch. There was nothing to prevent him entering, looking quietly around, finding Johnny Bull, waiting patiently till the right moment came and then tackling him once more.

But he almost turned and went away.

What finally prevented him, in spite of his almost overwhelming gloom, was some last remnant of curiosity. There were things about Johnny Bull that lacked answers. The scene in the flat that morning for one.

Why, he asked himself, had blonde, plump little Sandra been in such a state when she had answered the door? Had she got something to hide? Certainly his own arrival had seemed to upset her more than it should have done. And Johnny? What was it that he had not been able to find? Just his coat? Or something more important? The way little Sandra had crashed the heavy front door closed with such violence surely indicated that the pair of them had some secret. What was it?

Quietly he pushed the blank iron door wide enough open to slip through and went in.

He found himself in a long, bare, brick-walled, white-washed corridor, completely empty except for a row of three red fire-buckets hanging from iron brackets. He walked on tip-toe all the way to the far end. There, round the corner, were two successive pairs of swing doors with net-protected glass in their upper panels. He peered through.

Beyond a short wide corridor he caught a glimpse of what must be the recording studio itself, part of a wall completely covered in matt white sound-absorbent material and a microphone on a long boom. He could just hear the sound of music.

Very quietly he eased open the first pair of swing doors and went and peered again through the second pair. What he saw encouraged him. The studio was very large and was split up by square fence-like screens into various compartments. There were a lot of people about moving from place to place and busy with their own affairs. It should not be difficult to creep in and quietly observe what was going on.

Inch by inch he opened the second pair of doors and slipped through.

Inside he was struck first by the sheer volume of noise dinning through the air. He recognised the sound of the harmonium, and after a minute located the instrument he had seen in Johnny's flat. It was all by itself in an open-sided cubicle formed by three of the sound-proof screens. It was being played, not by Johnny as he had expected, but by a very serious-looking young man with heavy horn-rim spectacles, a mass of floppy hair and a brightly coloured beach shirt. And apparently something had been done to the instrument since it had left India: no harmonium that Ghote had ever heard could produce one quarter of the volume that this one did.

He took a long look round and spotted a corner that seemed to be unoccupied and which was partly screened off by the back of one of the cubicles. Quietly he made his way past the big sealed window of the control-room – he kept his eyes averted from the anxious-looking men stooping over the immense variety of knobs, switches and coloured lights – and over to his selected vantage point.

From its cover he was soon able to locate the blonde little Sandra. She was sitting on a red-leather bench against one of the walls talking earnestly with a stocky man of about thirty, who was distinguished chiefly for a short and very bristly beard. With so many people wandering about – young men tensely carrying clip-boards, girls in slacks looking as if everything depended on them – it took some time to spot Johnny Bull himself.

When at last he found the boldly handsome singing idol he saw that he was penned up in a smaller cubicle, it seemed, than anyone else in the big studio. His mane of dark hair was clamped down under a pair of huge, fluffy-eared headphones and, insultingly close to the chiselled features of his face, there dangled a black little microphone surmounted by an ominous cue-light.

A few seconds after Ghote had caught sight of him the music from the power harmonium reached a peak and the cue-light in front of Johnny jabbed a sharp red signal. Johnny winced visibly and began to sing.

'We gotta kiss that Kama Sutra way . . . '

His voice rolled out, deep, more tuneful than Ghote had expected, but somehow expressionless.

'There's gotta be a great love.'

He hung on to the note, though even Ghote could sense that he did so without the lingering affection for the sheer sound of it that the effect seemed to call for.

Suddenly the dying fall was interrupted by a brutal yell. Ghote saw after a moment that it came from someone who had already caught his attention, a short, dark-haired young man wearing a check shirt carefully buttoned to the neck, though tieless. He had been standing in his own cubicle, wearing headphones. But as he was up on a little rostrum he was able to see and be seen by everybody else in all the other fenced-off compartments. As the harmonium music had blared out he had been solemnly conducting it, marking each beat with such emphasis that he might have been attempting to teach nursery songs to a crowd of deaf children.

'Stop, stop,' he yelled.

He unclamped his headphones and let them dangle on his neck.

'We're getting nowhere,' he announced. 'Bloody nowhere. Everybody take five.'

Then he hopped down off his rostrum and was lost to Ghote's view. A moment later he appeared again, confronting Johnny.

'Now listen,' he shouted at him, in a voice which no one there could fail to hear. 'Listen to me. You're telling this chick something, see. Telling her, You've got to put that over. It's a feeling. A feeling. It's got to come from here.'

And with enormous vigour he tapped himself clearly and simply on the head.

'From here, see.'

Johnny swallowed and looked at him.

He mumbled something which Ghote could not hear. The man in the buttoned shirt answered more quietly. Ghote looked round to make sure that in the general movement that was taking place no one was too interested in his own quiet observation of the scene.

He decided he had better retreat temporarily to the depths of his corner.

And it was as he stood quietly there that he heard the three conspiratorial voices.

One he recognised at once as Sandra's.

'Look, tell me someone,' she was saying, with a plaintive wail, 'is he okay or not? It he doesn't make it after all

191

what I've been through, I swear I'll leave him. I swear I will.'

Ghote's antennae pricked up. All you went through? Had she gone through being an accessory to murder after all?

There was a chair just beside him, a tubular-legged plastic-seated thing. Cautiously he set it against the screen behind which he had heard the voices. He stepped up.

Peeping gently over, he found he was looking down on to the tops of three heads – Sandra's neat blonde one, the bristly one of the man he had seen before with the bristly beard, and the bald and shining crown of a big fat man wearing a bright blue suit.

The last was in the act of speaking.

'Never mind all that. He's got to make it. There's a lot of money tied up in that property.'

'Yes,' said the man with the bristly beard, 'but he's been between images. Wait till they see that new biog I sent out. It's pretty fabulous.'

Sandra turned to him sharply.

'Listen, Freddy,' she said, 'what's the good of a new biog, even if it is sensational, if he doesn't ever cut the disc?'

Freddy. Ghote's mind clicked. The publicist.

He surveyed the three heads beneath him.

'He'll cut it,' Freddy answered. 'The boys'll push him through. Look at some of the ones we've handled, the discoveries. Those chicks who couldn't sing a note.'

'But this one's got to be really good,' Sandra said. 'My Johnny needs a Top Ten.'

'Don't worry,' Freddy answered. 'Look, I'm telling the music press they get nothing more about anyone from me unless they use him big when the disc comes out. Colour pictures, definitely. And I'm going to plug it around so hard the jockeys won't know what's hit 'em.'

'But will he stand up to it?' Sandra said wailingly. 'You should have seen him this morning. Scared. Scared right through. And in the middle of it all I get a bloody Indian detective at the door.'

'An Indian detective?' Freddy asked. 'Could I use him? Rush out a quick hand-out?'

'No, you could not,' said Sandra, with the waspish tone Ghote recognised. 'You know what that creepy little man thinks about my boy? He thinks he's a bloody murderer.'

The fat man grabbed her elbow.

'You're saying Johnny's committed a murder?' he asked hoarsely.

'Don't be stupid,' Sandra said. 'Johnny's so doped with his opium he can't even murder a lyric, much less a real live girl. I had to put that pipe of his down the loo to-day, or I'd have never even got him here.'

Ghote stepped down off the plastic-seated chair. He did not need to hear any more. Sandra's unguarded words had painted the picture all too clearly. The last faintly promising line of inquiry had petered out. But the Peacock was still missing. Someone must have killed her. Could it still be the Smiths? Or had Robin some way of nipping out of his Nest unnoticed? Or had she been killed by a person or persons unknown? If so, he had entirely failed to find the least clue to whoever it might be.

Yet there must be something. Somewhere there must be something he had missed.

Sixteen

Next morning Ghote felt wretched. His head ached and his whole mouth felt abominably dry. He had been up till very late the night before attempting to deal with Superintendent Ketkar's paper and he imagined he was paying the consequences.

He had sat at the littered dressing-table, where not so long ago the Peacock must have sat at her school tasks, and he had held himself to it until he had read aloud and read again every single word Superintendent Ketkar had written, trying to recall just what it was the superintendent had said to him as he had gone through the same performance in the white-walled private ward at the J.J. Hospital ages ago it seemed. But the moment he woke up he knew that when in a couple of hours' time he stood in front of all the assembled delegates at the Drugs Conference the paper was not going to sound any better than it had as at about three o'clock that morning he had stumbled at last to the end.

He was not Superintendent Ketkar: that was all there was to be said. He was not Superintendent Ketkar, and try as he might he could not make himself sound like him.

He ate none of the big selection of delicious fried things Mrs Datta presented him with for breakfast. He drank some tea, but it did not seem to end the dryness in his throat. He left the Tagore House a lot earlier than he needed to.

On the way to the Commonwealth Institute in Kensington High Street he called in at the newsagents' near the restaurant. The back numbers of the papers he had ordered had arrived. He paid for them and took them outside to read, in spite of the low grey clouds overhead which threatened chilly rain at any moment.

He had not expected anything different, but when he found a full and clear account of the Smith brothers' brush with the law, confirming in every detail what he had learnt from their proud mother, he experienced a new access of rage against all the circumstances that had conspired against him from the very moment that Vidur Datta had flung himself in that ridiculous fashion at his feet at London Airport till yesterday's last disillusionment in the blaring, chaotic, self-absorbed Regent Recording Studios.

The Commonwealth Institute building with its fantastically-shaped, flyaway green roof, its sky-blue façade, its soaring white concrete struts, its neat rectangular stretches of ornamental water and the gay forest of tall flagstaffs in its forecourt did nothing to lift the dark twisted pleasure he had begun to take in the appalling mess he was about to make.

He plodded grimly round to the auditorium, thinking savagely of all the extra difficulties caused by having to read the paper in unknown surroundings.

And, just as he got to the auditorium entrance, a quite unexpected and somewhat ominous thing occurred. He sneezed. Once and violently.

It was only once, but it was enough. It accounted for his headache and his extraordinarily dry throat. He had caught a cold. He thought of the way he had had to stand, coatless, in that damp and green-moulded little area spying on the Smiths' house with the sharp hail beating down on him. That must be when it had happened.

If only it had been to any purpose.

Grimly he entered the auditorium. It was, if anything, more awe-inspiring than the hall at Wood Street police-station. Here, instead of a few rows of neat black leather chairs, there rose up a raked sweep of seats between tall matt-black walls ominously sprinkled with groups of spot-lights. They seemed to concentrate the whole auditorium like a crouching diver on to the narrow strip of the stage in front on which there was a very small table and just two chairs, one for himself and one for Superintendent Smart.

He stood letting the gloom soak deeply into him.

The other delegates, chatting animatedly together, took their places in the rows of steeply-raked, modish dark-grey seats. Ghote wished he could join them. How comfortable it would be to sit there and watch someone else perform up in the cruel light of the platform.

But instead he had to wait, alone and at every moment more panicky, for Superintendent Smart to come and lead him up on to the stage.

And nothing happened. The minutes went by and

Superintendent Smart did not come. The time the proceedings were due to start arrived and went, and still no Smart. Ghote, who had been dreading his arrival in case he made some cheerfully optimistic remark about the paper, now began to long for it as a prisoner in gaol longs for release.

At intervals of about a minute and a half he sneezed.

Glumly he looked towards the mass of delegates sitting waiting to judge him, and apparently quite unconcerned at the delay. In the very front row, relaxed and brimming over with vitality, was Superintendent Jaffer of Karachi. He was whispering something to his neighbour with a slight wink. The remark, whatever it was, provoked an uncontrollable roar of laughter. Ghote wondered whether he was being ridiculously touchy to suppose that he himself was the subject of the quip.

And still no sign of Smart of the Yard. And still at regular intervals those explosive sneezes.

Then at last relief arrived. Smart came suddenly bustling in, looking a little put out, peeling off his woollen gloves and pushing them into the pockets of his over-large stiff trench-coat.

He came straight up to Ghote.

'My dear Inspector,' he said, 'I really must apologise. The fact is I came up from Surrey by train and we got into Charing Cross nearly twenty minutes late.'

So much for this land of punctuality and regularity, Ghote thought bitterly. He might as well be back in Bombay.

He murmured something about the delay not mattering.

'But of course it matters,' Superintendent Smart said. 'To keep you waiting when you've got a paper to deliver. It's a nerve-racking experience at the best of times. Or at least it is for me.'

And he caught Ghote firmly by the elbow, gave him a smile of great sweetness and led him up the side-steps and on to the platform.

Then he went straight over to the little table and tapped on it for silence. As usual he secured instant quiet.

'Gentlemen,' he said, 'I will apologise only briefly for having kept you, and Inspector Ghote here, waiting. The main thing is to get on with our programme as I expect the paper we are to hear will provoke a good deal of discussion.'

Ghote found that the sweat on his palm had caused his hand to stick to the hard cover of Superintendent Ketkar's typescript. He peeled it away.

'However,' Superintendent Smart went on quietly, 'since this is our last day, I must take just a moment to extend to any one of you staying on after the conference a most cordial invitation to come and see the department at work at Scotland Yard. You have only to let me know.'

He looked up briefly and smiled.

'But now,' he said, 'there is no need for me to introduce you to our friend, Inspector Ghote. He is, of course, speaking to us with the voice as it were of Superintendent Ketkar.'

The voice of Superintendent Ketkar, Ghote thought. If only it was going to be.

He sneezed.

'Superintendent Ketkar,' Smart of the Yard went on, 'whose forceful analyses of the international dangerous drugs situation must be known to every one of you, is, as you have heard, laid up in Bombay. But we can feel he is with us in spirit to-day – in the person of Inspector Ghote.'

He sat down. There was applause. Ghote approached the little table. Three sneezes shook his whole body. He spread out Superintendent Ketkar's neatly typed, efficiently bound manuscript. He took a deep breath and turned towards the audience.

All along he had hoped that at this moment oblivion would mercifully descend.

It did not.

He sneezed again, and, hardly able through his watering eyes to make out the letters on the white paper in front of him, he began to read.

For five minutes he was listened to in intent silence.

He read a little, he stopped to sneeze, he read another phrase or two, he sneezed again. Twice realising he had made a slight mistake he went back a few lines. Once the second attempt was better. On the other occasion it was worse.

But after the first five minutes he began to notice from down in the body of the hall a series of slight sounds – rustling, coughing, even whispering – that indicated with chilling clarity that he was rapidly losing everybody's attention.

He ploughed on.

Words and phrases from what he was reading suddenly made a particular impact on him, and he let his thoughts dwell on them for a few moments. Then he discovered that he had no idea what it was that he was actually reading a line or two later.

The little hum of subdued chatter from the steeply-raked, grey seats rose gradually in volume. Ghote peered harder at his typescript. He read off another batch of words – 'considerable quantity of opium recently manufactured is still unaccounted for and it may be presumed that a proportion of this has found its way into illicit channels elsewhere.' A sneeze halted him. He pulled out once more his already sodden handkerchief, muttered an apology and went back to his reading.

'Opium recently manufactured is still unaccount – No, I am sorry. I have already read that. Please. Ah, yes. Illicit channels elsewhere, and it – '

Another catastrophic sneeze.

In the front row down below him he saw Superintendent Jaffer make absolutely no attempt to stifle the most enormous yawn. He had very large, very white teeth.

Ghote shut his eyes for one instant, forced them open again and returned to the paper. He read to the end of the page in front of him in a quick gabble, sneezed again slightly, turned over and read on.

It was only when he heard a distinct titter from the audience that he realised he had turned over two pages together.

He turned back and resumed.

The tittering grew. It was borne in on him that he had turned back not one but two pages and was well launched again into the saga that had caused Superintendent Jaffer to yawn so prodigiously.

He took out his handkerchief, blew his wretched nose with a long trumpeting sound, and, forcing himself to be calm, succeeded in locating the place where he was really meant to be. He read the next ten lines with something approaching fire. And then he started sneezing so continuously that all hope of keeping to this hardly-won level of achievement vanished.

But he ploughed on. He ploughed on and on, it seemed to him, for hours. Sneezes shook him and he stopped. He recovered, read a few lines more, and succumbed to sneezes again.

When he had got about two-thirds of the way through he gave up any attempt to correct mistakes he knew he had made. Instead he just read solidly on, not particularly emphasising any words but just saying them, getting them said and thrust behind him.

And at last, with his nose red and raw, with his throat sore and his eyes bleary, he came to the end. The last words were there at the foot of the last page, and he read them. He declined to make the gesture of looking up and even ever so slightly proclaiming them. He simply, and in a dry monotone, read them.

Then he straightened up from his stooping position over the frail table.

And a wonderful feeling of relief came over him. He had read the paper appallingly, totally appallingly, but he had read it. He had got through to the last word, the very last.

Facing him in the audience no one made a sound. The buzz of chatter continued. They had not realised that his task was completed.

And this did it. A sudden blaze of contempt for every single one of them and for everyone and everything else flared up in him. He lifted up his head.

'All right,' he shouted, 'ignore what I have read if you like. But drugs manufactured in Bombay are on sale in this very city. Everybody knows where to buy them. Even the singer Johnny Bull was able to tell me just where to go. Without a second thought, just like that. Drugs from Bombay: here. It is nothing short of a scandal.'

And then he turned, leaving Superintendent Ketkar's carefully planned and executed paper where it lay all pawed over and sneezed upon on the little frail table up on the platform, and fled.

The very sight of the people in busy Kensington High Street was more than he could bear. They all seemed so contented, prosperous, easy, strolling along with their big, brightly patterned shopping-bags, and their well-sprung, luxurious prams, talking together, laughing.

He hurried past, jostling people blindly, looking round for a way of escape. And then he caught sight of the wide open, black ironwork gates to Holland Park.

A park, he thought, on a chilly grey day like this. I should at least be able to get some peace there.

He wheeled abruptly and shot through the gates and on at a rapid pace till he was well inside the great walled-off area of the park, once the proud home of the Lords Holland and the Earls of Ilchester, now a public domain. And, as he had hoped, under the low grey skies with their already half-fulfilled promise of drizzle and dampness, there were only a very few people about to disturb the blackness of his mood.

On the broad walk by which he had entered there were two or three children on tricycles with gay coloured woollen hats and bright rainproof overalls. Elsewhere a solitary walker, mackintosh-wrapped and absorbed, strode through the greyness of the day. But otherwise he seemed to have the whole place to himself.

Stony-faced he tramped through a sodden rose-garden where on the bare spiny branches of the ordered rose-bushes two or three splodged pale pink or yellow blossoms still clung damply to their stalks. On the corner of a wall he saw a robin, a Christmas card robin with a neat red breast, perch momentarily in its search for worms in the damp earth of the rosebeds.

It served to remind him of the infuriating error he had been led into at the Robin's Nest café and of the humiliating and unpleasant events that had followed from it, through his encounter with the Smith brothers to the hailstorm which had given him this brain-shattering cold to that final moment of despair when he had read in black and white the evidence that the brothers had been safely locked up at the very time the Peacock had disappeared.

He kicked savagely at a pebble lying on the path, and missed.

He strode on through a gravel-pathed cloister where the loud echoing sound of his own steps sent him hurrying off again. He stared at the menu card outside a restaurant in part of the formerly huge Holland House. The prices on it astonished him.

A renewed burst of sneezing brought him, he did not quite know how, into an enclosed formal garden with precisely shaped flower beds each surrounded by an ankle-high little boxwood hedge. White-painted wooden benches, empty and upright, looked blankly on. Its very tidiness and air of placid permanence sent a new spasm of fury through his frame. The whole place seemed at that moment to sum up England for him, ordered, aged, quiet, affluent, formal, damp England. And he hated it.

How glad he would be in forty-eight hours' time when his plane was due to leave. Whatever troubles awaited him in Bombay, at least he would be putting his present miseries behind him.

He rushed through an ancient, wistaria-enwreathed

stone archway and out to a prospect of a big lawn, its grass dankly green and autumn-yellow, and heavy shrubberies surrounding it, the leaves of the bushes slowly dripping with the cold moisture in the air. His sneezing began again.

He saw at his feet a neat row of little dead-looking silver floodlights trained in a battery on some now flowerless shrubs.

To have so much money that you use artificial light to show up the beauty of flowers, he exclaimed angrily to himself. It was intolerable.

He stamped on.

At the far side of the big dank lawn a large bird, startled at the unusual sound of his steps, flapped its wings heavily and took to the air. He saw that it was a crow. But how different from the sun-warmed, boisterous, argumentative crows of Bombay. This creature's caw of remonstrance seemed like an ugly mocking laugh intended solely for him.

He smelt the rich, harsh odour of rotting leaves in his nostrils. He swung round and tramped off in the opposite direction.

And then it was that he saw them.

Under a trio of tall black-foliaged cedar trees, whose fallen spines carpeted the ground a dead brown, there they were: a pair of iridescent peacocks. The bright blue of their breasts caught his eyes infallibly, for all the distance between them. The colour spoke to him of India.

He moved quietly forward towards them. He saw that their plumage was past its summer best. Their long tails were a remnant only of their former glory. There would be no question of them suddenly turning, bowing slightly and setting up their great display fans. But it did not matter. The colour was there, shining, glossy, and with that peculiar simultaneous lightness and depth that seemed to him now the only proper way colour should be.

He got slowly nearer.

At last he was standing only three yards away from them, hardly daring to breathe in case they should be frightened away, lost in admiration of their courtly grace and of the shifting brilliance of their plumage.

And then the larger of the pair turned its beady eye sideways in a quick jerk and made a snatching peck at some morsel it had spotted. The sheer unreflecting greed of the action made Ghote actually wince.

It was perhaps the slight shock that was responsible. Or it may have been that at this moment his weary brain came to the end of a long half-unconsciously-followed trail. But whatever it was, he was suddenly aware that there in his mind, like a hard jewel, was the explanation of the disappearance about a month before from her home at the Tagore Restaurant, Hyde Park Terrace, London W.2 of a girl commonly known as the Peacock.

He spun round and, with his brain working furiously, made off at speed through the now unseen forlorn dampness of the misty park.

Seventeen

As Ghote, some half an hour after leaving the astonished peacocks in Holland Park, came rushing in at the back gate of the Tagore House Restaurant, he met the proprietor of that establishment making his way sedately and stolidly along the brick path through the cluttered yard towards him.

'Cousin Vidur,' he said, 'what luck to have caught you just now.'

Cousin Vidur looked at him and blinked.

'What is it that you wanted, Cousin?' he said. 'You seem to be very much out of breath. All this Western hurry. It is not at all the right way of going about things.'

'I wanted to ask you a question,' Ghote said.

'I am on my way to visit a wholesaler. But ask, ask.'

'I will,' said Ghote. 'Cousin Vidur, what has happened to the pictures that were in the Peacock's room, the pictures of Johnny Bull all round the walls?'

Vidur looked astonished.

'What pictures are these?' he said.

'The pictures she had of Johnny Bull, the ones with the titles of his songs written out underneath them. Your wife mentioned them the first evening I was here.'

Vidur shrugged his tautly plump shoulders.

'How should I know?' he said. 'I suppose the girl would have taken them with her, since she was so lovesick for this man.'

'She would have taken the one with the title "Going to My Lover To-day"?' Ghote snapped. 'No, Cousin, that she did not take. Because you used those words in the farewell note you pretended she had left, Cousin.'

Vidur's solidly plump face went pale.

'What does all this mean?' he said without conviction.

'It means that after you killed her you found she had by chance provided you with what looked exactly like a farewell note in her own writing,' Ghote answered. 'I have only worked it out in these last few minutes. I had seen the note and later I saw the title of that song on the walls of Johnny Bull's flat. My visit there was not so useless after all. But until I thought of you as the one who killed the Peacock I had no reason to connect the two things.'

'Why did you think of me?'

Vidur managed a little truculence.

'I thought of you,' Ghote confessed, 'because I was watching a pair of peacocks just now and one of them suddenly made a peck at some disgusting morsel on the ground, and I realised that proud birds can be greedy creatures too. As the Peacock was. A dazzling and gay creature, but greedy also. I thought of all those clothes she had, so many that a lot were left behind. Where did she get the money for them all, I asked. And the answer was that she got it from you.'

'I would not give a girl like that money to buy prostitute's clothing.'

Vidur darted a proud glance from side to side.

'But you had to,' Ghote said. 'She had found out, just as I did, that you take opium, and she demanded money from you till one day she tried your proud spirit too far.'

And then Vidur did collapse. Just like a pricked balloon.

Ghote swung away from him.

'Is she buried under all this rubbish?' he asked, nodding his head at the piled high rotting crates and mouldering cartons that completely hid the ground of the little backyard.

'Yes, she is there,' Vidur said.

'You left yourself in a very awkward situation all the same,' Ghote said. 'With your wife so devoted to the girl, you were in the position of having to do much more than the little you would have liked to find out why she had left home.'

He laughed sharply.

'I ought to have known that early on,' he said. 'From the way you behaved at the airport. Something was bound to be wrong with the proud Vidur Datta getting down on his knees and kissing my feet. There was something that certainly did not ring true.'

Vidur looked at him. All the hard plumpness in his face had sagged away. But in his little eyes there was still a strain of fierce calculation.

'Cousin Ganesh,' he said, 'what are you going to do with me? We are cousins, remember. And we are Indians also in this appalling country together.'

'Do with you?' Ghote answered with simple certainty. 'I am going to hand you over to the proper authorities.

Indian or British, a killer is a killer and the police are the police.'

And, as if by magic, at that very moment the high wooden gate of the backyard opened and the silver-topped tall blue helmet of a Metropolitan Police constable appeared round it.

How he had come to be there Ghote could not imagine. But he saw that at this juncture he would be useful indeed. Always provided he was a reasonably intelligent man. Heaven forbid that he should turn out to be another prejudiced joker like the sergeant at the local station, or, worse, a pompous old idiot like his advice-laden rescuer at the Smiths' house. He would see.

'Constable,' he called. 'Just the man I want.'

'Inspector Ghote?' the constable said. 'We were wanting you too, sir.'

He darted his head back through the gate and called something out. A moment later Detective Superintendent Smart came into the little backyard, craning out of his stiff trench-coat and rubbing his woollen-gloved hands hard together.

'Inspector Ghote,' he said briskly, 'we hoped we might find you here.'

'Well,' Ghote replied, 'I do not know about that. But I am certainly glad to see you. I have a murder suspect for you.'

Superintendent Smart's head came half an inch farther out of the tortoise-necked collar of his stiff coat.

'Murder, is it?' he said cheerfully.

'I do not think there will be any difficulty securing a conviction,' Ghote said. 'If you will get your constable to take charge of the fellow, I will come along and explain all about it.'

Superintendent Smart's eyes twinkled and he gave his woollen gloves an extra brisk rub.

'This is the girl who disappeared, is it?' he said. 'I heard about that. So it was an inside job, eh? They were very foolish to invite a chap like you on to the premises. That's two crimes you've cleared up inside an hour.'

'Two crimes?'

'Yes, indeed. Your information about that fellow Johnny Bull knowing where opium was sold was just the tip we needed. We made a few inquiries and we've got him. He brought in heaven knows how much of the stuff in an old harmonium, if you please.'

He gave a dry little chuckle.

'That'll be something to tell old Ketkar when you see him,' he said.

And a great warm rosy light invaded Ghote's whole being. Never mind how he had done it, but he had pulled off a double. He had dealt with the extra burden that had so unfairly been placed on him on his visit here, and he would also go back to Superintendent Ketkar in unexpected triumph.

An enormous grin spread slowly across his whole countenance.

Superintendent Smart gave a quick rub to his gloved hands.

'Well,' he said, 'I hope you're going to give yourself a fine old treat in the rest of your stay here. You've certainly earned it. What's it going to be? A slap-up tour of all the sights? You haven't had much time for that, I bet.'

Ghote thought of his postponed visit to the Tower. But it no longer held the glamour for him that it had done on the first day of the conference. A lot of changes had occurred in his outlook since then, none bigger than in the last few minutes here in this rubbish-piled backyard.

'No,' he said, 'I do not think I want to see any sights of that sort. What I would like to do, if I may, is to take advantage of your kind offer and come and see you at work.'

And on Detective Superintendent Smart's weather-beaten tortoise-face there appeared a little pink flush of pleasure.

'My dear chap, we shall be delighted.'

'I will be with you early to-morrow,' Ghote said. 'Just as soon as I have got my wife a little present. A souvenir of Britain for myself also. It will not take long to get. I know just what I want. It is a teapot, most handsome and what is called, I believe, reasonable.'